NEVILLE'S QUEST

1754: Thomas Neville has resigned his commission in the twenty-second of foot to sail to the Americas in search of his sweetheart, Emily — sold into slavery by the evil Reverend Cruikshank. Neville and his small band of ex-soldiers fight their way past pirates on the high seas and see off a French expeditionary force on Georgia's frontier — only to find that, together with her friend Leila, Emily has made good her own escape. On their return to England they face highwaymen, grave robbers, thugs and traitors — yet Neville's greatest challenge lies in declaring his feelings for the woman he loves . . .

Books by Ken Holdsworth
Published by The House of Ulverscroft:

THE FINAL CURTAIN
POSSESSED

KEN HOLDSWORTH

◆

NEVILLE'S QUEST

Complete and Unabridged

ULVERSCROFT
Leicester

First published in Great Britain in 2012

First Large Print Edition
published 2012

The moral right of the author has been asserted

British Library CIP Data

Holdsworth, Ken.
  Neville's quest.
  1. Historical fiction.
  2. Large type books.
  I. Title
  823.9′2–dc23

  ISBN 978–1–4448–1029–5

Published by
F. A. Thorpe (Publishing)
Anstey, Leicestershire

Set by Words & Graphics Ltd.
Anstey, Leicestershire
Printed and bound in Great Britain by
T. J. International Ltd., Padstow, Cornwall

This book is printed on acid-free paper

1

Off the coast of South Carolina Colony, 1754.

Out on deck it was ominously quiet. I had become so used to the continuous creaks and groans of a tall ship under sail, the constant slapping of waves against the bow and the raucous cries of the seabirds flying alongside, that I had grown not to notice any of it, until now, when, suddenly, it wasn't there anymore.

The silence was unnatural, almost frightening. The huge sails hung limp and impotent, and apart from an almost imperceptible roll, the ship was motionless. We were becalmed.

I made for the poop deck to see what was being done to get us underway. 'Come on!' I growled through clenched teeth as I climbed the steps. After almost sixteen wearisome weeks at sea we were actually in sight of the coast, and here we were, going nowhere! 'Come on! Let's get there!'

I suppose it was the sensation that time was standing still that caused me to feel in my waistcoat pocket for the timepiece I was carrying there.

Each time I looked at it I couldn't help but admire the skill of the clockmaker who had made this slim golden orb with its mother-of-pearl, three-handed dial. Unlike a carriage clock, 'watches', as they have begun to be called, are carried on one's person, therefore providing knowledge of the hour wherever you are. They were fast becoming a fashion accessory but were, in my opinion, a vain extravagance that even with all the wealth I had attained in India stood low on my list of priorities. This one had come into my possession purely as the result of a foolish wager, a wager I wished to God I had never won.

The watch had belonged to Tobias Bloom, a successful young merchant with his two feet planted firmly on the ground. I met him just after I'd jumped ship at Fort St George, the British East India Company's trading post at Madras. Sometime later, when he was visiting me at Dunmere Hall, my family's home in Cheshire, he bet his gold watch against my dog, Hagar, that there was no substance to the story that the Reverend Edwin Cruikshank was possessed by an evil spirit, and furthermore, because the arrogant cleric was dying of consumption, the demon within him had its eye on my young brother, Giles, as its next host.

'The answer's as plain as a pikestaff, old boy,' Tobias had said with a laugh. 'All you have to do is make sure your brother is well out of the way when Cruikshank breathes his last, and then, with no one to jump into, this demon, evil spirit, or whatever you want to call it, will jolly well have to expire with him, eh, what?'

By a perverse twist of fate Cruikshank had died in Tobias's arms and subsequently the young Jew, formally a deeply religious and a most gregarious person, had become a recluse, haunted by thoughts that were both lewd and misanthropic.

The Bloom family traded with the colonies and it was they who arranged passage to the Carolinas for my little expedition.

Our ship was to sail from the Pool of London. On arriving at the nation's capital, I had presented myself at the Bloom family's waterfront offices. With the formalities completed, I ran up the stairs to the third floor, where Tobias had his living quarters.

When I got there I was shocked to find him confined to his bed following a massive seizure, brought on when he had tried to enter his Synagogue.

My ship was about to depart so I was forced to leave him and when we reached the Thames estuary, the pilot cutter brought the terrible news that he had jumped to his death from his bedroom balcony.

It also delivered a package that had been found on his bed. It was addressed to me and inside, wrapped in my silk kerchief (which I had left behind after mopping his fevered brow) was his gold watch.

It was Tobias's way of telling me that I'd been right about Cruikshank.

★   ★   ★

The sun was warm on my back as I climbed the steps to the poop deck. Suddenly, there was a cry from the lookout.

'Sail ho!'

'Where away?' bellowed the officer of the watch.

'On the starboard beam,' came the reply.

The ship's officer strode past me, snapping open his spyglass as he did so. He was the second mate, a genial West Countryman by the name of Saunders. He had been at sea long enough to be the master of his own vessel and it was my guess that his natural good nature had been the drawback to his career. Merchant adventurers prefer their masters to be tough and uncompromising, like our own Captain Jensen.

I followed him to the taffrail, and I saw her,

4

a tall, three-masted barque, materializing like a ghost out of the fogbank. It's true the sun was burning away the fog that had shrouded us during the night but she seemed to be moving.

Saunders echoed my thoughts. 'She's found a bit of wind. Look, there's a bow wave,' he said enviously. 'Just a minute! Her gun ports are open.' He lowered his telescope. 'My God! She's flying the black flag.'

The helmsman took one hand off the wheel and crossed himself. 'Holy Mother of God,' he whispered.

'Mr Gabriel!' Saunders shouted. 'Pipe all hands and send someone to fetch the captain.'

There were two shot-firing, swivel guns mounted one on each side of the poop deck's wooden taffrail, put there no doubt to be used by the ship's officers in the event of a mutiny. One was within reach of where I was standing. Like the rest of the vessel, it looked to be in good order. I asked Saunders if there was any other armament on the ship.

He groaned audibly. 'The *Caprice* is built for speed, Major, not for fighting. She can outrun just about anything on the sea — but only when her sails are full.' He thumped a clenched fist into his hand. 'The captain will skin me for taking her too close inshore and losing the wind.'

The ship's company began noisily to fill the main deck below us. Among them I saw the Miller family, the only other passengers, and my travelling companions, Daniel Coggins and Archie Fowler, both former British East India Company soldiers and now part of my small expedition.

George Miller, a man in his forties, was sailing to the colonies with Mary, his wife, and his two daughters, Sarah and Jane. Their quarters were between decks and Miller was paying part of the cost of passage by working as a deckhand so I didn't get much opportunity for conversation with him. However, my valet, Barney Nolan, a perpetual fount of information, told me that Miller's wife was expecting another child, the daughters, Sarah and Jane were aged fifteen and thirteen respectively, and with one thing after another going wrong for Miller in England he was hoping to change his luck by taking his family to the New World and start a new life.

Nolan appeared with my sword. Like Coggins and Fowler, he had also been a soldier, a lance corporal in the twenty-second and my batman in that regiment until I bought him out when I resigned my commission to come on this enterprise.

Immediately following him was the tall figure of Captain Jensen, looking every inch the Viking that no doubt his forefathers had once been. Jensen stared hard at the pirate ship, his blond beard bristling and his ice-blue eyes glinting with anger. If it were possible to sink a ship with a look, that barque would have gone straight to Davey Jones's locker there and then. Turning to his second mate, he said sarcastically, in heavily accented English, 'How is it, Mr Saunders, that this pirate is sailing north like us, yet he moves and we do not?' He spoke so coldly his words sent a shiver down my spine. I could just imagine how Saunders felt.

I suddenly had an idea, and before the second mate could think of an answer, I said, 'About your cargo, Captain.'

My interruption visibly annoyed him. 'Make your point, Major,' he snapped.

'You are carrying something that could prove very useful under the circumstances.'

'And what is that?'

'Muskets Captain. Ten boxes I believe? You mentioned it at dinner.'

Jensen turned his attention away from Saunders who took the opportunity to wipe the sweat from his brow with the cuff of his shirt. 'Yes, for Harwood's Militia,' he said, now looking at me with interest. 'And bayonets also.'

'Do you have powder and shot?'

'We have.'

'We can't run, so we have to stand and fight. Do you agree Captain?'

He smiled. 'You have plan, Major?'

'How many in your crew are former soldiers?'

'I ask them,' he said, and turning to face the assembled ship's company, he shouted, 'Step forward, any man who has been in army!'

There was an immediate movement among the men on the deck and over a score of them pushed their way to the front of the assembly. I noticed with some interest that one of them was George Miller. I called for anyone who could load and fire a musket to join this group.

The captain was quick to spot that there was some reluctance in responding to a request from a passenger. 'You see what is there!' he bellowed, pointing at the pirate ship. 'We must fight that devil!'

'But we've got no cannons!' someone shouted.

'Major Neville has plan. Do as he says and we keep our freedom. But we must be quick!'

More hands moved forward, doubling the

original number of volunteers.

'Take over Major,' he shouted for the benefit of the ship's company. Then, dropping his voice so that only I could hear him, he added, 'And for everyone's sake this plan of yours better be good one, *ja?*'

Saunders was standing behind us. I spun round and told him to detail twenty men from those still standing at the rear of the deck to go down into the hold and bring up all the wooden boxes labelled 'Land Pattern Muskets'.

'I want them up here on deck at the double,' I said. 'And the boxes of bayonets as well — and bring all the powder and shot you can carry. Quickly now — go!'

The second mate looked at his captain who gravely nodded his head in consent. He hurried away, no doubt relieved to be away from Jensen's chilling look. My next job was to send the bo'sun to fetch the sail maker. I needed a waist-high storm canvas fastened along the whole length of the starboard rail.

The lynchpin of my plan was my valet. Having assisted me to buckle on my sword belt, he was standing by awaiting further orders. I called him and he snapped to attention. Nolan was not used to being a civilian.

'I want forty muskets in two ranks on the starboard side, Mr Nolan,' I told him. 'I want them out of sight when the pirate ship closes in, and well back from the rail until the enemy's grappling hooks have taken hold. They are then to move forward keeping below the canvas screen that the sail maker will soon be rigging up. You're familiar with volley firing; you've done it enough times in the twenty-second. Tell your men what's required of them and get them to load their muskets as soon as the second mate gets here with them . . . And Nolan?'

'Sir!'

'Get those females below deck.'

When those with experience of musketry were making their way forward I saw a man start to move with them, only to change his mind halfway. I now pointed to him and asked his name.

He stood up straight and squared his shoulders. He wasn't a big man but he was tough and sinewy and looked as though he could hold his own in the fo'c'sle. 'Chambers, sir,' he replied, almost belligerently.

'Haven't I seen you sitting on the capstan playing a fiddle?'

'Aye, sir, that you have.'

'When I called for men who could load and fire a musket you started to come forward but you changed your mind. Why was that, Chambers?'

'Never had no training with muskets, sir,' he said. 'I learned myself how to shoot, with my father's fowling piece.'

'What did you do before you went to sea.'

'I were a poacher, sir,' he called back defiantly. 'The magistrate gave me the option of service with the King's navy or the rope. That were more than ten year ago and I been at sea ever since.'

'D'you still keep your eye in with a gun?'

He grinned. 'That I do, sir. It don't matter where we drops anchor, Cookie always looks to me to bring him back something for the captain's table.'

I could see that my two former East India Company soldiers were itching to receive their orders. I was about to assign them to their stations when the boom of a cannon echoed across the water. This was followed by a great splash forward of our port bow throwing up a tall plume of water.

Archie Fowler could contain himself no longer. 'That blighter's out to sink us, Major,' he complained angrily.

I'd heard much talk of pirates during my time as an impressed ordinary seaman on His Britannic Majesty's sixty-gun, ship-of-the-line, *Indefatigable*. The general opinion in the fo'c'sle seemed to be that pirates would slaughter a whole crew to the last man but

11

they'd go to any length to preserve their ship and its cargo.

'He'll not do that,' I shouted down to him. 'He'll try and board us. When the muskets arrive, you and Chambers take two apiece, with plenty of powder and shot, and get aloft. You're our best shot and Chambers should be pretty good as well. He was a poacher and poachers learn to bring their quarry down with the first shot or their families go hungry. Pick a couple of nimble lads with a knowledge of firearms to take with you as loaders. Then, in your own time, you are to shoot anyone on the pirate ship who seems to be giving orders — but don't start shooting until you hear me give the first order to fire. Right?'

'Who'll be in charge when we're up there?' Fowler asked cunningly.

'You, of course.'

His little ferret-like face beamed. 'Right, Major,' he shouted and began pushing his way through the crowded deck calling out, 'Come on Chambers fall in, jump to it!'

Fowler's comrade-in-arms was a heavily built man with a badly-healed sword cut on the side of his face that furrowed his cheek and twisted up the corner of his mouth so he seemed to have a permanent leer. I pointed to the dozen or so men that hadn't yet been assigned a task. 'Coggins, form those men into a bayonet detail. When the two ships meet, your job will be to deal with any would-be heroes who jump the gap or swing across it on ropes.'

He gave me one of his lop-sided grins. I'd seen Daniel Coggins in action with a bayonet and I remember thinking at the time that I was glad he was on my side.

Saunders' party arrived on the main deck with the six-foot wooden boxes, plus some smaller ones that I guessed contained the bayonets. Eager hands levered off the tops and the contents were swiftly distributed.

The pirate ship was now only yards away and closing fast. The hair on the back of my neck was telling me that we were being watched through a spyglass so I shouted to everyone to keep the weapons out of sight.

Fowler and Chambers grabbed the first of the powder and shot to appear, and with two muskets apiece slung across their backs they scuttled up to the tops. Their loaders carrying more powder and shot quickly followed them and soon they were all lost from sight amid the sails.

I looked for Coggins and his bayonet party and saw him with a half-dozen big, determined-looking men kneeling at the ready behind the hatch cover on the port side of the main deck, each of them gripping a five-foot musket with a wicked looking seventeen-inch bayonet attached.

The coxswain was at the helm and Morgan, the first mate, had joined his captain on the poop deck. Jensen stood immobile watching the pirate get ever closer to his unarmed ship, the knuckles of his right hand white as he gripped the hilt of his sword.

'We must stop them, Major. If we die, we die quick, with sword in hand, ja? If they get hold of woman and girls, they die slowly, understand?'

Saunders reported back, red-faced and breathless. I complimented the second mate on completing such an arduous task so quickly, calling on Jensen to agree, which he did, albeit grudgingly.

'I have another job for Mr Saunders,' I said. 'If that's all right with you, Captain.'

'Is part of plan?' he asked and I nodded. 'Take him,' he said disdainfully. 'I have no need of him.'

I steered the sweating second mate over to the starboard swivel gun. 'I want you to load this monster, light your fuse but keep it out of sight. When I give the order to fire, point the gun down at the main deck of the pirate ship and put the fuse to the touchhole. Then reload and fire again at will. Got that?'

'Aye, sir,' he said, and surprised me by

adding, 'I'll not let you down, sir.'

'I'm sure you won't, Mr Saunders.'

'The captain's angry 'cos I got us becalmed,' he moaned. 'But in that fog I thought it best to hug the shoreline. I knows this coast, Major. I've sailed it more times than the captain and Mr Morgan put together! All the settlements along the shore lights look-out beacons at night so's their night watch can see if any natives are a-creeping up on 'em — it were bad luck the wind dropping like that, but that could've happened to anyone.'

'I'm sure your only concern was for the safety of the ship, Mr Saunders. I have every confidence in you.'

He smiled, touched a knuckle to his forehead and hurried away to fetch powder and shot for the big muzzle-loader.

The captain walked across. 'Well, Major Neville?' he said grimly. 'I see you have men in position. What you want me to do?'

'I'd like you to put all hands not under arms to work, Captain, reefing a foresail or something. Make it look normal.'

'Anything else?'

'Strike your colours.'

His eyebrows went up. 'Strike — my — colours?' he repeated, looking puzzled.

'Yes, haul down that flag on the jackstaff.

The pirates will take it as a sign of surrender.'

Light dawned and he nodded his large leonine head in agreement. 'Mr Morgan!' he shouted to the first mate. 'Send someone to bow and remove company flag. Be quick now!'

Our sails were stirring sluggishly in a light breeze that had arrived too late. There was very little water between the two ships now and I could read the name, *Avenger*, painted boldly on the pirate's prow. Her motley crew of naval deserters and runaway slaves lined the port rail three to four deep, shouting and waving their swords and pistols. A great cheer went up from them when our flag was lowered. Some jokers even climbed onto the rigging to hurl insults at us, each pearl of verbal abuse producing a burst of raucous cheering from the murderous-looking assembly below.

It wasn't long before grappling hooks were thudding onto our deck and the ropes attached to them hauled in. As the barbed claws bounced and scraped across the planking, Nolan's men followed them, crouching low in order to stay hidden behind the canvas-lined rail. The hooks eventually took hold and the order to 'heave away' was shouted. The pirates' jeers and catcalls were louder now and I could feel my heart

16

pounding in my chest as the two ships were brought closer together. When there were just a few feet separating us, I called out, 'Front rank, make ready!'

The first line of men behind the storm-canvas straightened up into a kneeling position, bringing their muskets to rest on the top of the rail. They took aim.

'Fire!' I screamed.

The volley was a little ragged but it had the desired effect. The shots tore through the surprised pirates, those in the forefront waving their limbs in the air like marionettes jerking on invisible strings before falling forward into the rapidly narrowing gap between the ships.

'Front rank, retire and reload!' Nolan bellowed.

On my right, Saunders' swivel cannon boomed, scything a huge, bloody swathe through the tightly packed men on the *Avenger's* main deck, while from aloft came the twig-snapping crackle of my sharpshooter's muskets, dropping one man after another on the enemy's poop deck. There was some sporadic fire from the pirates and I saw one of Nolan's men fall. A few pirates, who were either very brave or just plain foolhardy, did swing across the gap on ropes slung from their yards but these were speedily dealt with by Coggins' bayonet detail.

The front row of our musketeers had moved back leaving a clear field of fire for the second row, which was now standing and waiting for the word of command. I noted that Nolan had stepped in to fill the gap in the line. 'Rear rank, make ready,' I shouted. Their muskets came up into the firing position at the shoulder.

'Fire!'

Twenty muskets thundered in response and more pirates went down. Saunders' swivel gun boomed again, adding to the smoke and the acrid smell of gunpowder that now filled the air.

With Fowler and Chambers having taken out just about everyone in command, the enemy was now in a state of disarray and confusion. Men ran blindly in all directions, their only thought to get away from the relentless rain of fire that was slaughtering them in great numbers.

I feared that some of them would find their way down to the gun deck and once there get the idea of firing one of their cannon point-blank at us, if only out of spite.

'Coggins!'

The big man looked up from wiping the blood from his bayonet and grinned. There was nothing this man liked more than a scrap.

'Yes, Major?' he shouted back.

'We're going to board her, Mr Coggins. Bring your men up here and we'll go over the taffrail.'

'Yes, *sir!*' he shouted enthusiastically.

'Front rank ready, sir!' came from Nolan who was standing looking up at me from the main deck, his cheek blackened with powder and his eyes shining with excitement.

'Fire!' I yelled, and more pirates went down. 'Give the order to fix bayonets, Mr Nolan and take your men over the side. The enemy's ship is ours. Drive the murdering bastards into the fo'c'sle. And make sure you clear the gun deck. Shoot anyone you see with a lighted fuse in his hand.'

Coggins' bayonet party had joined me on the poop deck. I had soldiers around me again. My ears rang with the noise of battle. Powder smoke drifted before my eyes, its familiar smell filling my nostrils. My heart was pounding. I was in my element.

I drew my sword. 'Come on, Coggins,' I shouted. 'Let's finish it!'

19

2

Saunders was put in charge of a prize crew to sail the *Avenger* into harbour, and a proud sight she made too, with *Caprice's* spare Union flag fluttering from her stern.

Jensen said he'd only given his second mate the job to keep him out of his way, but I viewed his decision to follow the barque closely as it sailed upriver as an acknowledgement of Saunders' superior knowledge of the waters hereabouts, in particular the location of the sandbars that lined the deepwater channel all the way into Charleston.

The town stood on the eastern bank of the river, a fortress surrounded by marsh and bog. Fine houses and churches lay within its protective walls and I was instantly reminded of my first sighting of Fort St George, the British East India Company's trading post at Madras.

Because of our draught, both ships were forced to anchor in deep water. Having told Nolan to pack our bags and get word to Coggins and Fowler to do the same, I went to find the captain to arrange for a boat to take my party ashore. I found him in his day cabin bent over the chart table. He had a map spread out in front of him.

'See how the town lies at junction of Ashley and Cooper rivers,' he said without looking up. 'This is good map. Every inlet and creek is clearly marked.'

I peered over his shoulder. ''A Plan Of Charles Towne',' I said, reading the heading.

'It is for sure 'Charles Towne'. Named after your King Charles — the one whose head you English didn't chop off.' He laughed heartily at his little joke. 'But everyone says, 'Charleston'. Is sailor's talk, Major. Is like saying bo'sun for boatswain. Soon folk are writing it down as such, I bet you . . . Now, Major, you want to go ashore, eh?'

'I *am* eager to get started,' I said.

He stood up, a serious expression on his handsome face. '*How* long has it been since your sweetheart was put aboard that slaver — two years is it?'

As I nodded grimly the memories came flooding back.

★   ★   ★

When he discovered she was carrying his child, the Satanist, Edwin Cruikshank, had arranged for my Emily, a beautiful mulatto, to be taken aboard a slaver bound for the

21

colonies. It was while searching for news of her in the seedy taverns of Liverpool's dockland that I got snatched by a Royal Navy press gang and forced to work as a common deckhand on HMS *Indefatigable*, bound for India. I jumped ship at Fort St George, Madras, and with the help of Robert Clive, a former school friend and by then a person with much influence in that part of the world, I got back to England — only to find that not only had Cruikshank reduced my father to a drunkard, seduced my mother and taken over the family estate, but that he also had evil designs on my younger brother.

Yes, it had taken all of two years. But now, Cruikshank was dead and I was free at last to find my love.

★ ★ ★

'Will you let me have a boat?' I asked.

Jensen smiled sympathetically. 'I send Morgan ashore for harbourmaster. You can have ship's pinnace when he gets back. Come, we go on deck and wait for him together, eh?'

The harbour was full of small craft. I looked for the jolly boat and caught sight of it as it was leaving a pier that bridged the marshy ground between the town and the

22

river. With its four powerful oars dipping in unison it was closing on us rapidly.

Jensen handed me his telescope and I put it to my eye. I could see the first mate at the helm and seated next to him was a small man dressed rather incongruously in drab clerical black. There was another passenger sitting facing them, his scarlet coat proclaiming him to be a soldier. He had a huge ostrich feather in his black cocked hat, which I thought a bit ostentatious. For the life of me I couldn't think of a regiment in the British army whose officers affected such a gaudy decoration.

'I send Morgan to bring harbourmaster,' Jensen repeated. 'I need barges to take cargo ashore.'

I didn't ask about the soldier. I assumed he was coming to take charge of the prisoners.

The uninjured pirates were securely battened down in the *Avenger's* forward hold and our ship's surgeon had gone across with the prize crew to do what he could for the wounded. The screams of the amputees could be heard quite clearly across the water as he went about his bloody business.

'What will become of the pirates?' I asked.

'White men will be hanged as warning to others,' he replied unemotionally. 'Black men will be sold as slaves to work on plantations.'

'And the ship?'

'Ah,' he said with a grin. 'We sail *Avenger* back to London and there she will fetch good price I think. You shall have your share Major Neville; never fear. But first I must sign on crew for voyage.' He stroked his beard thoughtfully. 'Ordinary seamen are no problem, go to any port in world and you find plenty men looking for berth. No, the difficulty will be finding captain at short notice.'

'Why not Saunders? He's got the experience.'

Jensen expelled his breath in a derisory manner. 'Yes, he should be master of his own ship but he is, what you say? Soft-hearted.'

'Then put Gabriel with him,' I said. 'Promote him to first mate if necessary. They can run the ship together. With Saunders' sailing experience and a tough first mate taking care of good order and discipline you'd have the ideal combination.'

He mulled over the idea, a wry grin slowly spreading across his face. 'I suppose it could work . . . damn it, Major, I have now to find new bo'sun!'

Fowler and Coggins appeared on deck with their baggage, which they dumped next to a large valise that I hadn't noticed before but now recognised as mine.

In the time it took for Nolan to reappear

with his own gear the jolly boat had come alongside and Gabriel was giving orders to lower a scrambling net to enable the passengers to climb on board.

Jensen hurried forward to meet the harbourmaster and the military man. Morgan effected the introductions and the four men talked together for a moment before Jensen beckoned to me over to join them. The little harbourmaster surprised me by stepping out from the group and grasping me firmly by the hand.

'Alistair Mackay,' he said enthusiastically. 'And I'm right honoured to meet you, Major. The captain says it was your military tactics that defeated those pirates.' He stepped aside and waved a hand in the direction of the soldier. 'This here's Colonel Harwood. He'll be wanting to hear all about it I'm sure.'

While the harbourmaster was speaking, the military man had been busily checking his coat for any dirt it may have picked up climbing on board. The garment sat on his shoulders beautifully, and although I thought the braiding was perhaps a little overdone I couldn't help admiring the skill of the tailor who had made it.

He straightened up and regarded me appraisingly. He was a tall man that I judged to be in his early forties. His face was fleshy with an unhealthy, dissipated look about it. Beneath the impressive hat, he wore a peruke with side curls and a pigtail, a style fashionable in some regiments.

An overdressed dandy he may be but I gave due deference to his rank. 'Colonel,' I said, holding out my hand and putting on a friendly smile. 'I'm Thomas Neville. Are you here to take charge of our prisoners?'

He ignored my outstretched hand. 'I'm here, sir,' he said haughtily, 'to take charge of my goods, which, I understand, you have been making free with.'

Colonel Harwood. Harwood's Militia, of course! I remembered the captain saying the boxes of muskets and bayonets were *en route* to them.

'We really had no choice if we were to defend the ship,' I reasoned.

He was singularly unsympathetic. 'If I am to defend this colony, Mr Neville, I need good weapons. My men have been making do with rusty hand-me-downs for long enough. I insist that each and every one of the muskets I ordered from England is rigorously inspected. I'll not pay for damaged goods!'

Captain Jensen intervened. 'Has been done, sir,' he said amicably. 'They are cleaned and oiled and repacked in original boxes. There was one gun damaged — by sword cut

— and I replace it with musket from ship's armoury. We carry six, all new this voyage.'

'Steel ramrod?'

'Of course.'

Jensen waved his hand in the direction of the still open door of his cabin. 'Gentlemen, we go to my room, eh? Mr Morgan will fetch ship's manifest . . . we all drink little rum, *ja*?'

He made to follow his visitors but catching my eye he hesitated, and turning to Gabriel, who was still standing by the rail, he ordered him to take my party ashore. Then, grasping my hand firmly in his, he said, 'Go to Marine Tavern, Major. Is simple seaman's inn but accommodation is clean and landlord is honest man.'

★   ★   ★

A short time later I was standing on Charleston's wooden pier together with Fowler and Coggins surrounded by our belongings. I hardly had time to realise that Barney Nolan was missing before that admirable servant reappeared with a handcart to wheel our baggage to the inn.

Jensen had gone on to describe the Marine Tavern as being built with stone brought as ballast to Charleston from Bermuda. This had led me to expect something out of the

27

ordinary but in fact it turned out to be one of many similar houses in a narrow dockland street that, apart from the unusual pinkish look of the stone, could have been anywhere; Bristol, Liverpool, or even Black Town, Madras for that matter. Gaudily dressed, painted 'ladies' stood outside rival establishments competing with each other with shouted words of enticement to the many groups of noisy sailors weaving their drunken way over the cobblestones.

Leaving Barney Nolan guarding the luggage, I went inside and was immediately reminded of Josh Napper's cosy tavern in the little hamlet of Goostrey, on my family's estate in Cheshire. Josh was Emily's father, and he had been with Finch, my head groom, and me, searching for her in Liverpool's dockland on that fateful night when I had been carted off, an unwilling and unconscious new member of His Majesty's navy.

I was to learn later that the publican, having got Finch to agree to look after his tavern, had himself sailed off to the Carolinas in a desperate lone bid to find his daughter.

Yes, the Marine Tavern could well have been his. The large smoke-filled room was just the same, packed with men of all ages shapes and sizes sitting at long, scrubbed, wooden tables putting the world to rights over a drink. Occasionally there would be raised voices but this was usually followed by laughter. There was even a jovial innkeeper with a clutch of foaming pots in each hand, chatting to his customers as he squeezed between the tables. I grabbed hold of him when he came within reach.

'Joshua Napper,' I said. 'Do you know him?'

He wriggled his arm out of my grip. 'Yes, I know Josh,' he said guardedly.

My heart leaped. A lot of water had passed under the bridge since Emily's father had left for Carolina and I liked to think that Josh had found his daughter and was running an establishment of his own, right here in Charleston perhaps. I knew deep down that it was only make-believe but it had kept me sane since I got back from India. Was I about to be told it was true?

'He's done work for me,' the innkeeper continued. 'He's a tinker — and he's a good 'un.'

Josh a tinker? Never! The Josh I knew was a man who liked his creature comforts. There was no way I could picture him as an itinerant repairer of pots and pans. But on second thoughts, the job would allow him access not only to the kitchens of the plantation owner's grand houses but also to the humble living quarters of their slaves. Yes, it would be an ideal profession for a man searching for a daughter sold into slavery.

Slavery! The very word made me shudder. The thought of Emily as a slave had been my constant nightmare for the past two years. I forced myself to think constructively and I asked the innkeeper if he knew where Josh was.

'I haven't seen him for months,' he said. 'He'll be somewhere up country like as not.'

While I was talking, big Daniel Coggins, with little Archie Fowler trailing in his wake, pushed his way through the standing customers to the far side of the room where a long table stood before a row of barrels draped with wet towels. I remembered, back in England, Emily explaining that wet towels were an attempt to keep the ale inside the barrels cool. I guessed they were being used here for the same reason. Emily would stand at a similar table in her father's tavern busily filling tankards from a large jug that she replenished regularly from a tap on one of the barrels. Here the same job was being done by a youth who, although he seemed to be as efficient as Emily, was not as pleasing on the eye.

In no time at all, Fowler and Coggins were laughing and joking with the other patrons. I heard the word *Avenger* mentioned and suddenly there was a hush and all heads turned in my direction. Then there was general shouting and cheering and I was urged along with hearty slaps on the back until I was standing with my companions, each of them holding a foaming tankard in one hand and a small glass of some colourless liquid in the other.

I don't remember paying for any drinks or how many I had during that jolly occasion; in fact I don't remember anything at all until Nolan awakened me the following morning.

'Good morning, Major,' he said cheerfully. 'I've brought you a dish of tea. Drink it down, sir, it's said to reduce the effects of alcohol.'

I was lying on a soft bed in a small attic room fully dressed, boots and all. A swift check confirmed that my money belt was still under my shirt and my pistols were still in the pockets of my coat. I sat up quickly and then, as a bolt of pain shot through my head, I wished I hadn't.

It was hard to remember the last time I had slept right through the night. On the *Indefatigable* my insomnia had been due to a sadistic bo'sun but since then it was because my mind had been so active in making plans, firstly to rid my family of Edwin Cruikshank and then to mount this expedition to find Emily.

There was a jug standing in a basin on a small washstand. I went over and splashed some water on my face and dried myself on a towel that Nolan produced as if by magic. I asked him where the rest of the party were quartered.

'I'm in the room next door, Major. It's as small as a snuffbox, so it is, and it doesn't have a window — but it does have a door, which is something I suppose. Coggins and Fowler are in an old bakehouse out at the back. The inn is full you see, with having Colonel Harwood's men here.'

'Harwood's Militia?'

'There you have it, sir. Come to collect the muskets and ammunition from the ship. The innkeeper is happy because the colonel is paying for their accommodation. Apparently if they was regular King George's soldiers he'd be expected to board them at his own expense, so he would.'

My face must have registered concern because he added, 'Don't you worry about us, sir, my room is quite adequate, and I've been down to have a look at the bakehouse. It's clean and dry and the lads have got palliasses filled with sweet-smelling straw to sleep on, and plenty of blankets . . . And there's a pump in the yard just outside their door, so there is.'

Feeling that some fresh air would help to clear my head I went downstairs to see these makeshift sleeping quarters for myself.

3

The bakehouse was a small, stone-built, lean-to tacked onto the back wall of the inn. Coggins was seated on a cask outside its door smoking his pipe. On seeing me, he made to get up, the familiar lop-sided grin on his ugly face. 'That colonial ale is strong stuff eh, Major?'

Motioning him to remain seated, I asked if he was happy with his billet.

'I've slept in a lot worse, sir,' he said amiably.

On looking inside I reckoned the room to measure roughly eight feet by ten, and, as you would expect from its designation, there was a large brick oven that took up almost a third of the floor space. A diffused light came from shuttered windows, one in the front wall by the door and the other at the far end beyond the oven. However, it was dry and the straw-filled palliasses looked clean and comfortable.

The little Cockney was lying stretched out full-length on one of them. Catching sight of me peering in, he quickly scrambled to his feet.

I told him I'd been concerned for their well-being but now I'd seen their quarters I was happy to let the arrangements stand, adding that no doubt when the militia had collected their muskets they would be moving on anyway and then there would be other rooms available, should we need them.

Fowler snapped his fingers as a thought occurred to him and began pulling on his boots. 'Our bleedin' muskets and ammunition are still on the boat, in that big trunk what's in the hold,' he said. 'It may 'ave been brought ashore by now. Dan and me will go and fetch it if you like?'

I agreed, and feeling better for being in the open air I said I'd go with them, but first I would have to find Nolan and arrange for him to follow us with the handcart.

I eventually met up with the two former East India Company soldiers in the cobbled street outside the tavern. They were talking to some men who, although now uniformly dressed in black tricorne hats, red coats and thigh-length, deerskin gaiters, I recognised as our drinking companions of the previous evening.

Archie Fowler was particularly eager to introduce to me to one of them.

'This 'ere's Obadiah, Major,' he said, giving a gangling youth with a spotty face a playful punch on the shoulder. 'We sank a few between us last night, eh Obie?'

'I can see you're all soldiers but where are your weapons?' I asked him.

Before Fowler's new friend could open his mouth, one of the men, a corporal, stepped forward, and answered for him. 'This squad's on loading duty, Major. Corporal Logan's squad is the one with muskets.' He grinned. 'They're seeing your pirates off to the lock-up.'

★ ★ ★

There was much activity at the landing stage. A flight of seagulls circled the air above a fishing smack that was landing its catch, their raucous cries forming a background to a melodious work song being sung by a gang of black men who were carrying sacks from a wagon and loading them into a sailboat. Their supervisor, a sandy-haired man with a cudgel stuck in his belt was trading good-natured banter with a couple of lightermen busily tying up their vessel.

This craft had obviously just arrived from the *Caprice* as in it I saw my trunk and the wooden boxes containing Colonel Harwood's muskets. Another barge, moored on the other side of the pier, was disgorging a motley group of dejected-looking prisoners from the *Avenger*.

A number of townspeople had gathered to watch the former buccaneers shuffle towards the lock-up, the men of Corporal Logan's squad speeding up any would-be dawdlers with shouts and the sharp end of their bayonets.

The impatient snorting and scraping of hooves from the horses and the laughter and squeals of children as they chased each other between the wagons added to the symphony of sound.

The colonel himself, in all his finery, was there, talking to Mackay, the little harbour-master, and Captain Jensen.

A shot rang out and Harwood fell to the ground.

Suddenly there was pandemonium. The prisoners cried out in alarm, thinking the soldiers were firing on them, women in the crowd screamed and anxious parents ran out to gather up their children.

Then someone yelled, 'There he is, behind the wagons!'

I swung round and I saw him, less than a hundred yards away and still holding his gun. He was a thickset man and apart from a scrap of cloth covering his nether regions he was completely naked. His face was streaked with paint and there were feathers stuck in his hair. Another musket fired. This time it *was* one of the soldiers, aiming at the native. The shot missed and the man leaped into the swamp below the pier.

'Get after him, Fowler,' I shouted. 'He's heading for that island beyond the bastion. I'll run along the wall and cut him off.'

It was then that Harwood scrambled to his feet. The colonel retrieved his magnificent hat, which fortunately for him hadn't gone into the river, and held it up for all to see. He waggled a finger though a hole in its brim.

'Look at my hat!' he said bitterly. 'I had that sent out from England. It didn't come cheap, let me tell you.'

'He's as rich as Croesus and he worries about the cost of a hat,' Obadiah whispered to Fowler as they stripped off their coats.

'An inch lower and it would 'ave been 'is 'ead,' I heard the little Cockney reply as they set off after the would-be assassin.

'But you fell, Colonel?' Mackay was shouting. 'We all thought you'd been shot!'

Harwood dusted himself down. 'A soldier's instinct, sir,' he said grandly. 'Always hit the ground at the first sound of gunfire.'

'He'd have been a fat lot of good at Arcot,' Coggins grumbled. 'You wouldn't see Captain Clive diving for cover when the guns

38

went off. He'd be standing up there in the thick of it, urging his men on with shot buzzing round his head like angry bees.'

Robert Clive was Daniel Coggins' hero. The big man had fought with the former East India Company clerk at the battle of Arcot four years earlier when, with only two hundred men, Clive had beaten a combined French and Indian force of over fifteen thousand.

'Right, Coggins. Come with me,' I said. 'And mind what you say about Colonel Harwood. Don't forget he holds the King's commission.'

We set off at the loping run I'd been introduced to by an old sergeant in the twenty-second who had served in the American colonies some ten years earlier. He claimed the natives could maintain it for hours and still fight a battle at the end of it. I tried it and I believed him. The stride was longer and slower than the British Army's regulation 'double time', enabling a body of men to cover ground quickly but also silently and without getting seriously out of breath. I quickly saw its benefits and introduced it to the men under my command both in England and India.

'No disrespect to you, sir,' Coggins said, falling into step at my side, 'but Colonel

Harwood is typical of them what looks down their noses at East India Company officers.'

As is the custom among the gentry and nobility, my father bought me my first commission in our county regiment. Officer's commissions were only available for purchase in British infantry and cavalry regiments. The thinking behind this was simple. It ensured that those in command of the military would be from privileged backgrounds and therefore less likely to support revolution or insurrection. This system did not operate in the army of the Honourable East India Company, which resulted in its officers not being regarded as gentlemen by many a King's man, officers and soldiers alike.

With Coggins but a pace behind me, I ran to the end of the pier and then scrambled down onto a narrow strand of hard sand and shingle that ran along the base of the town wall. I could hear Fowler and Obadiah whooping and shouting to each other somewhere off to my left as they ran through the swamp in pursuit of the native. Our paths must have been convergent as by the time I reached the bastion I could see them quite clearly. They were soaking wet, covered in mud and loving every moment. I looked for their quarry. He wasn't very far ahead of them and seemed to be tiring. It wasn't long before I heard a jubilant shout followed by a loud splash signalling that he had been apprehended.

I halted at a spot where the hardstanding was at its widest and waited for the would-be assassin to be brought in. The hunters arrived breathless and triumphant, dragging the man between them. He was a sorry sight. The proud feathers were gone from his long, iron-grey hair, which was now matted with blood. His body was that of a man well past his prime, and he was fatter than I would have imagined a hard-living savage would be.

The wound on his head didn't look serious. I asked Coggins to help me turn him on his back.

'I don't know why you colonials call these fellows 'Indians',' he grunted, taking hold of the native's shoulders. 'I was in India four year and these 'uns don't look like any Indian I've ever met.'

Obadiah laughed. 'Blame Christopher Columbus for that,' he said. 'He was so cocksure he could get to India by sailing westwards that when he made landfall he straightaway called the inhabitants 'Indians' not realising he'd only got as far as the Bahamas.'

The unconscious man rolled onto his back with a groan.

I gasped. 'If you've got your flask with you Coggins, let me have it now.'

'It's against the law to give an Indian liquor, Major,' Obadiah whispered.

'This is no Indian,' I said, 'American *or* Asian. This is an Englishman. This is Joshua Napper, Emily's father.'

4

I unscrewed the top of the flask and gently dribbled some of its contents between Josh's lips. He coughed and his eyes flickered open. As consciousness flooded back, he struggled to sit up, looking around fearfully. On seeing me he relaxed.

'By all that's merciful, Master Thomas, it's you,' he exclaimed. 'I've prayed for this day and now my prayers are answered.'

Although still on the heavy side, Josh had lost a lot of weight since leaving England, and beneath the now sadly comical streaks of warpaint his once plump and jovial face now looked drawn and haggard.

I relieved Coggins of his coat and despatched the big man with instructions to return with some clothes and boots for the former innkeeper.

Draping the warm outer garment around Josh's naked shoulders I asked him what the devil he was doing masquerading as a native and taking pot shots at Colonel Harwood.

The light came back in his eyes. 'I saw him fall,' he said eagerly. 'Did I kill him?'

'No, thank God. You only put a hole in his

hat. Why on earth do you want to kill the colonel? What's this all about, Napper — and where is Emily?'

Josh drew the coat around him and lay back against the wall with a sigh. 'Emily is what it's about, Master Thomas. And when you've heard what that cockalorum did to her, you'll want to shoot him yourself, you see if you don't.'

Fowler and Obadiah were standing off to one side and I could hear the little Cockney quietly explaining to his newfound friend just who this 'naked savage' was.

'I'll always be grateful to your father for taking me on as a tenant,' Josh continued. 'And I feel real bad having just up and left the farm like that — but when I found that Emily's ship had sailed, the only thought in my mind was to go after her.'

Josh had been one of my father's 'good works'. The farm needed a tenant and Josh, a widower with a young daughter, had needed work. It was only a small farm, barely large enough to support a family, but it was in the centre of the village and so, with my father's blessing, Josh had turned the big old farmhouse into an inn. This had proved extremely popular with locals and visitors alike, and quite lucrative for Josh.

'Don't worry about the farm,' I told him.

'It's being well managed in your absence, and as for my father, he's, er, had other things on his mind.'

Josh looked relieved at that, and for the first time he smiled. 'I told 'em at the docks I was a farmer, so I got a berth looking after the ship's livestock, feeding and watering 'em, and mucking 'em out, that sort of thing. Then I'd slaughter and butcher 'em as needs be on the voyage.'

I shuddered. Not the sort of job I'd relish, but then Josh came from farming stock that couldn't afford to get sentimental over their animals, and at least it got him a free passage.

'When I got to Carolina I really didn't know where to start,' he continued. 'There seemed twice as many black faces there as white.'

'I was told you became a tinker.'

'What money I brought with me soon ran out so I had to get a job — but it had to be one where I could travel around and keep on a-searching. I knew how to mend a leaky kettle and rivet a new handle on a cooking pot well enough, so I set myself up as a tinker.'

'And Harwood?'

'I wore out three pair of boots going from plantation to plantation and I'd just about given up hope when I found her.'

'Emily?'

'Bless you no, Master Thomas, a West African woman at the Harwood plantation who'd recently arrived from England. Her overseer was a black who'd been here since he was a boy. He spoke her lingo so I was able to talk to her through him, if you understand me? She told me she remembered a young English girl being bundled in next to her when her ship put into Liverpool docks. From her description it could only have been my Emily. She said Harwood had bought them both at the auction.'

'And is Emily there now?' I said excitedly. Josh laid a restraining hand on my arm.

'Hold your horses, Master Thomas. She's not there and never was. Harwood grows rice on his plantation. Not that he does any of the growing himself. His slaves to do that for him . . . They say it was the slaves what taught the white settlers how to grow rice, and now it's one of the most important crops in the Carolinas.'

'Get on with it man!' I said irritably. Instantly regretting my impatience, I moderated my tone, asking again where his daughter was.

He straightened up and looked me in the eye, the muscles of his jaw twitching in anger. 'Emily's quite safe, Master Thomas. I knows exactly where she is and I'm on my way to fetch her home — but I had a score to settle with Harwood first. I'll tell you why, and when I'm done, you see if you don't want to shoot the bastard yourself.'

We couldn't leave until Coggins got back with the clothes so I squatted down next to the former innkeeper.

'The plantation brings in the money,' he began, 'but Colonel-pretty-boy-Harwood doesn't reside there. Oh, no, he's got a grand house here in Charleston, with his family's coat of arms carved in the gateposts.'

'He comes from a noble family then?'

'His father's Earl somebody-or-other.' Josh turned away and spat on the ground. 'He might live like a lord, but him being the third son the chances are he'll never be one.'

Having grown up believing that most of the great families in England are related, I shuddered at the thought of that puffed-up popinjay being a cousin, however distant!

Josh's eyes were glinting angrily. 'He likes to decorate his Charleston house with beautiful young women too,' he said. 'For the amusement of his posh friends, when they come to his gaming parties.'

I was horrified by the image that was beginning to form in my mind. 'Emily was one of them?' I ventured.

'Apparently he snapped her up at the slave auction, her being almost white.'

'But she was with child?'

'She were wearing loose clothing and her condition wasn't detected for some weeks.'

'But it was eventually?'

Josh lowered his head and his shoulders shook. I didn't say anything, feeling that it was better for him to let it all out. Eventually his sobbing subsided and he was able to carry on.

'There's a well in the back yard of Harwood's mansion,' he said, 'where the water is drawn up by a donkey working a treadmill.' He looked up, his eyes still brimming with tears. 'When he discovered Emily's condition, Harwood apparently went into a rage, shouting that he'd been cheated out of his money.' He paused and then, with his voice a barely audible whisper, he added, 'The bastard replaced the donkey with my Emily.'

I was horrified. 'But what of her child?'

Josh sat in silence for a moment. 'A child *was* born,' he said at length. 'Emily gave birth in a stable like an animal.'

'Or like Mary in Bethlehem?' I suggested.

He obviously hadn't thought of that and he looked up at me and nodded with a grateful smile. 'The only one to help her was a half-witted white woman by the name of Leila Sculley, a pot washer in the kitchen. The child only lived a few days.'

My God, he was right! At that moment, all I wanted to do was race back to the pier and finish the job he had bungled. I took a few deep breaths to calm myself down. 'Where is she now?' I asked.

'Savannah. When the child died, this Leila helped her to bury the poor little bundle behind Harwood's stables and then they set off together for Georgia.'

'Isn't that the new colony?'

'Yes, General Oglethorpe's. Been going now for nigh on twenty year.'

I'd grown up listening to the coffeehouse talk about James Oglethorpe and the thirteenth colony. To some he was a philanthropist who had set out to make a haven for England's poor in the Americas where there would be no strong drink or slavery, but to others he was simply a soldier of King George creating a buffer zone between English South Carolina and Spanish Florida.

'How do we get to this Savannah?'

'I was going to go by boat, Master Thomas. That was to be my next step — after I settled my account with Colonel Harwood.'

There was a crunching in the gravel behind me. I turned to find Coggins grinning down

49

at us, and behind him was Nolan carrying a bundle of clothes.

'Sorry I've been so long, Major,' the big man said. 'But I bumped into Barney here, so I helped him take the trunk from the *Caprice* back to the inn. I've brought one of my shirts and spare pair of breeches for the, er, gentleman.'

'Dan thought his boots would be too big,' Nolan added, regarding the painted 'savage' with amused interest. 'So I brought a pair of mine. I trust your man here will only be needing them temporarily like, as I'd appreciate having them back . . . '

'These clothes are just to get him to the nearest outfitters,' I said, shaking some coins out of my purse. 'See he's properly kitted out, Nolan, and you can have your boots back.'

My valet hadn't finished. 'I was also given to understand he could do with a bit of a wash, sir,' he continued. 'So I've taken the liberty of bringing a damp facecloth and a towel.'

The two former soldiers seemed to know exactly what was required so I left them to it and set off for the pier with Fowler and Obadiah. On the way I asked the little Cockney why he was looking down in the mouth.

'Well, we caught the bloke, didn't we, sir?'

he grumbled. 'Only now we'll 'ave to look like a pair of idiots and say he got away.'

Before I had a chance to respond, Obadiah broke in with, 'But if we don't let on he wasn't an Indian, Archie, no one will think twice about it. An Indian would know these swamps like the back of his hand and if that fella had really been one we wouldn't have stood a chance. He'd have melted away like a ghost.'

If Obadiah hadn't suggested keeping Josh's identity secret I would have, so I was only too pleased to fall in with this suggestion. Fowler shrugged his shoulders resignedly and went on to tell his friend how he had helped run Josh's tavern in Goostrey for a few days after the innkeeper had gone off to the colonies.

Having left the pier in a state of pandemonium the transformation that greeted me on my return was remarkable. The prisoners had gone, presumably to the lock-up, and with nothing left to gawp at, so had the gallery of onlookers. The boat being loaded by the melodious slave gang had sailed, leaving the fishing boat and the second lighter from *Caprice* the only vessels still tied up there. The latter, now relieved of its cargo, rode high in the water and rocked gently at its mooring.

Captain Jensen was still there. The big Viking was in conversation with Alistair

Mackay, or I should say listening to the garrulous harbourmaster who seemed to be the one doing all the talking. With a passage to Savannah uppermost in my mind I went up and interrupted them, perhaps a trifle rudely, with a cheery 'Hallo.'

'Major Neville!' Mackay exclaimed. 'Did the Indian get away? That doesn't surprise me. Never mind, there's no harm done . . . Unless you count the hole in the Honourable Colonel's expensive hat.' With that he burst out laughing.

'Is Colonel Harwood quite recovered from his fright?' I asked.

He dismissed the incident with a wave of his hand. 'Yes, yes,' he said, still chuckling. 'That darned redskin did him a service. I was just telling Captain Jensen here that I've no doubt the colonel will dine out on his miraculous escape from death for months to come.'

I turned to Jensen. 'As you know Captain, the object of my expedition is to find a young woman who was forcibly taken into slavery. My latest intelligence tells me she is in Savannah, in Georgia. If it's not too much to ask, Captain, could you take my party with you and put us ashore there.'

The Norwegian rubbed his beard. 'Nothing is too much for the man who save my ship and cargo — and possibly my life also, but from here, Major, ships sail north to England. Savannah is to the south.' Then he smiled. 'I have transferred my cargo to *Avenger* and she is ready to sail. It will take days, perhaps weeks to arrange another cargo for *Caprice*. The *Avenger* has a large cutter. If Captain Saunders is agreeable, you can have it. I can provide men to sail it.'

That Saunders should be referred to as a captain was evidence that Jensen had accepted my recommendation and put him in command of the *Avenger* for the return trip to London. I asked if this also meant that Gabriel had been promoted to first mate.

'Yes, it does,' he replied. 'And I make Chambers bo'sun of *Caprice* in his place. He is, what you say, a loner? This not a bad thing for a bo'sun I'm thinking. He was for many years a seaman in your Royal Navy. He's not a big man but he's tough and the crew respect him.' Jensen looked well pleased with himself. 'He'll come soon with the jolly boat to take me back to *Caprice*. Come with me, Major, and we stop at *Avenger* on the way'

Bo'suns have to be strict disciplinarians and in spite of his name, Gabriel was no saint — but neither was he a sadistic bully, and God knows I'd suffered at the hands of one of those! No, Gabriel was fair and just, and in

53

my opinion well deserving of promotion. As for Chambers, his appointment surprised me but on reflection I decided that Jensen had chosen wisely, as some responsibility would perhaps knock the chip off the former poacher's shoulder and he'd be a better man for it.

Fowler ambled across to join us. I asked him what had become of Obadiah.

'He's gone running after his mates,' he said. 'We was talking to them fishermen and they told us they'd seen a Frenchie ship landing troops south of some river with a funny name, something like 'ha-ha'. Obie seemed to think it was important and he went chasing off to find the militia.'

'The Altamaha?' Mackay suggested.

'Yes, that's the one. Funny name ain't it?'

'It was the name of a Yamasee Chief,' the little harbourmaster told him. 'That river is Georgia's southern boundary. It divides the British colony from Spanish Florida. I don't like the sound of French troops disembarking there. No gentlemen, I don't like the sound of that at all.'

Jensen beat me to it with, 'If they land south of river, then are they not on Spanish territory?'

Mackay nodded. 'Aye, that's correct, Captain, but it's too close to Georgia for comfort. They'll be up to no good; you mark my words. For some months now the French have been stirring up trouble between the Indians and the settlers in the backwoods of Virginia, and in New England too.' For a while he was silent, a worried look on his face, and then, jutting his chin out defiantly, he added, 'But if they dare cross the Altamaha they'll have the Highlanders to answer to.'

This time I got in first. 'Highlanders?' I asked.

'Aye, they're the bravest of fighting men and legendary for their fierceness in battle. General Oglethorpe brought them from the Highlands of Scotland, to defend his colony.'

The jolly boat was tying up and Captain Jensen turned to go. 'Then there is no problem, Mr Mackay,' he called back. 'Your Scotch Highlanders will deal with the French.'

I saw the harbourmaster flinch. 'We prefer to be called Scots, Captain,' he called after him. ''Scotch' is what the *Sassenachs* call our whisky.'

5

Saunders received us right royally on the *Avenger*, even going as far as having Jensen piped aboard. When he saw me his ruddy face beamed. Stepping forward and raising his hat politely, he said, 'Welcome aboard, Major Neville. A bit more shipshape than the last time you trod this deck, eh?'

'And the welcome is a mite friendlier,' I replied with a laugh.

'Please join me for a glass,' he said, sweeping his hat towards the day cabin. 'To wish me luck with my first command.'

We followed him to the large room beneath the poop deck. A long oval table stood in front of the floor-to-ceiling windows. This was where the captain studied his charts by day and where the ship's officers would eat at night. Now, a wide-bottom decanter and a half dozen glasses stood on its polished surface. Saunders busied himself pouring the drinks.

'I will have one glass, then I must return to *Caprice*,' Jensen said. 'The major has favour to ask you.'

Saunders handed me a glass. 'Just say the word, Major.'

'I was hoping you'd lend me your cutter.'

He looked surprised. 'Fancy doing a bit of sailing, do you?' he said incredulously.

The big Norwegian laughed and told him of the plan.

'You can have the cutter with pleasure,' Saunders said. 'The darn thing takes up too much deckroom anyway.' The smile left his face and he looked pained. 'But I can't spare any sailors to crew it, I'm afraid. I'm well short of a full compliment as it is.'

Jensen swallowed his drink. 'Just get the boat in the water, I provide the men. I send them over when I get back to *Caprice*. Their first job will be to take Major Neville ashore.' He started to leave and then, changing his mind, said, 'Perhaps I will have one more glass Captain Saunders. We have wished you successful voyage, now we drink to Major Neville's good hunting, *ja*?'

Saunders gave orders for the cutter to be lowered into the water and rigged ready for sailing. He then joined me on deck to wave goodbye to Jensen. We stood together at the rail watching the pinnace as it was rowed back to the *Caprice*. A few moments later I saw it return with two seamen standing proudly in the stern, the promised crew for the *Avenger's* cutter. When they got nearer I was pleased to see that Captain Jensen had

57

sent me Chambers, his new bo'sun. The other seaman I recognised as being a member of Coggins' bayonet party.

I thanked Saunders for the use of the cutter and congratulated him on his promotion.

'I wouldn't have got it if it hadn't been for you, sir. Mr Gabriel told me that.' He grasped my hand. 'Good luck to you, Major, and I hopes you find the person you're looking for.'

Chambers and the other seaman, a lean, sinewy man who later told me his name was Dennis (whether that was his Christian name or surname I was never to discover) took over the cutter, and with the former poacher at the helm we fairly flew back to the pier.

'I see you got the *Avenger's* cutter, Major,' Fowler shouted down as we were tying up. 'Who's that sailing it, is that Percy Chambers?'

Some names suit people. Had I been asked to wager on Chambers' given name I would have gone for one of the Apostles. The weather-beaten face grinning up at us looked to me more a James or a John than a Percy. 'Yes, Chambers is the new bo'sun of the *Caprice*,' I called back. 'And Captain Jensen has put him in charge of getting us to Savannah. So, go back to the Marine Tavern at the double and tell our party to get ready to sail.'

'You can tell 'em yourself, Major,' Fowler

grinned, 'they're all here.'

I climbed up the short ladder attached to the side of the pier to find the rest of my expedition was there waiting for me. Big Daniel Coggins was perched on a mooring bollard smoking his pipe with the others grouped around him.

Josh Napper was there, smartly clad in an Indian-tanned buckskin shirt and trews, which he wore with a low-crowned, wide-brimmed hat. Because of a sprained ankle (the result of being jumped on in the swamp by Messrs Fowler and Obadiah) he was leaning on a smart Malacca cane. This added to the image, no doubt intentionally contrived, of the well-to-do colonial settler.

It was understandable, I suppose, that he would want to look his best to meet his daughter but I intended that my party would dress more simply, in clothing I considered to be practical for the task ahead.

We went back to our quarters where I gave Chambers some money with instructions to obtain food and drink for the journey. I then told Coggins. Fowler and Nolan to parade in half an hour with their bags packed and wearing the thick, homespun shirts, thorn-proof breeches and the buttoned, thigh-high, calico gaiters, much favoured by the military, that I had purchased for us all in London.

We all met at the appointed time and made our way back to the waterside.

My first stop was at the shipping agent's office. There, having first removed the four muskets and all the powder and shot it contained, I arranged for the trunk to be sent back to the Blooms in London to await my collection.

I didn't like the look of the shipping agent and came away feeling uneasy.

Nolan set off to return the cart to the tavern while the rest of us proceeded to the end of the pier

Later, as we were loading our backpacks into the cutter, there was a shout from the town end of the pier. A group of stevedores offloading some baulks of timber from a wagon moved aside to allow two scarlet-coated figures in full marching order to pass. One waved a hand; it was Archie Fowler's friend, Obadiah. The other was a junior officer I hadn't seen before, a slightly built but determined-looking young man in his early-twenties. Taking the smartly dressed Josh Napper to be in charge of our party, the officer went up to him and doffed his hat.

'Major Neville? Colonel Harwood's compliments, sir. We are to accompany you to Savannah.'

Obadiah tugged his sleeve and pointed to

me. 'Begging your pardon, sir. But this here's the Major,' he said, pronouncing 'here's' as 'he-yah's'.

The young ensign swung round to face me. He made no apology for his error. 'We are tasked to observe the French and ascertain their intentions,' he said. 'If they *have* crossed the Altamaha, I am to send word back immediately. The militia could well be needed to defend Georgia.

'But General Oglethorpe's Highlanders . . . ' I began.

'Marched westward over a week ago, sir,' he replied. 'To where Georgia borders on French territory. It's the colonel's opinion they were deliberately drawn away to leave the southern boundary undefended.' The young officer then raised his hat to me. 'Ensign Lacoste, sir,' he announced.

'That's a bleedin' frog's name,' I heard Fowler say to Coggins in a stage whisper.

Lacoste heard him. 'Yes, it *is* French. My grandparents were Huguenots from Brittany.' He drew himself up. 'But I am second generation Carolinian,' he said proudly. 'You have Huguenots in your country too, do you not, Major?'

I was embarrassed by Fowler's rudeness. 'Indeed we do,' I said, 'and a very skilful and industrious people they are too. They have established such a thriving silk cloth industry in London's Spitalfields that the area is commonly referred to as 'weaver's town'. In fact, the street where they built their first church is called Threadneedle Street.'

Lacoste smiled. 'You are familiar with that part of London, Major?'

'No, but the mills of Macclesfield, in my home county of Cheshire, supply it with thread.' Then, giving Fowler a stern look, I added that my forebears were also from France, deliberately omitting to say that the original de Nevilles had come over with William the Conqueror.

Lacoste saluted me by touching the brim of his hat with his finger before walking away to add his knapsack to the bags being passed down to Dennis in the cutter.

I drew Obadiah aside and asked him how much Ensign Lacoste knew about our mission.

'Only that you are seeking your sweetheart from England, sir,' he said. 'He doesn't know she's a runaway slave.'

Much relieved, I told him I'd be grateful if he left it like that. I had been blithely referring to Emily as my sweetheart but in my heart of hearts I knew that the innocent girl who once drew the line at a surreptitious kiss in her father's stables could never be the same again. She had been seduced by the Satanist, Edwin

Cruikshank, subjected to the horrors of a slave ship, treated abominably by Colonel Harwood, given birth to a child in the most primitive of conditions and then suffered its loss. I dreaded to think what state of mind must she be in. I dearly wanted to be reunited with her and to bring her home. But would she want to come? Would she even be pleased to see me?

I had a lot of questions for Josh that simply wouldn't wait, so when we went aboard I made a point of sitting next to him.

'I take it you know where Emily is residing in Savannah?' I asked him.

The former innkeeper was looking more like the old Josh I used to know. His eyes twinkled and there was big smile on his round, rosy-cheeked face. 'That I do, Master Thomas,' he replied. 'Her and Leila Sculley are working at an orphanage there.'

That sounded like good news to me. 'Tell me more,' I said enthusiastically.

'As soon as I was told that Emily was at the Harwood mansion,' he began, 'I set out for Charleston. I was over the moon. After almost two years of searching, the thought that I'd finally found her was almost too much to bear.' He turned to face me. The smile was gone. 'Then I saw an advertisement in the local paper that said, 'Colonel

63

Harwood offers to pay a forty shilling reward plus reasonable expenses for the return of Emily, his runaway slave'. It described her as a comely young mulatto who speaks excellent English, and could easily pass for being white. Well, that was her, wasn't it? My Emily. The advertisement went on to say she was thought to be in the company of a white, female indentured servant, one Leila Sculley.

'I went straight round to the mansion and them below-stairs told me the whole tragic tale.'

'So how did you track her to the orphanage?'

'That was thanks to George Whitfield, the preacher. He was due to be holding a big open-air meeting in Charleston that same night. I wasn't really expecting to find Emily there. If she had any sense she'd be in hiding somewhere, but I went along anyway.'

The mention of open-air preachers set me thinking of John Wesley, and how he had preached in my home county of Cheshire, from the steps of the *Roebuck* tavern in Knutsford and the *Red Lion* at Holmes Chapel. While Josh was filling his pipe, my thoughts moved on to the night I couldn't get near the fire in Josh's tavern because the arrogantly handsome Reverent Edwin Cruikshank was standing there, one booted foot on the hearth, holding court before a motley collection of slack-jawed yokels who were drinking in his every word. Never had anyone witnessed a cleric speaking within the warmth of a taproom — and paying for everyone's ale as well!

On that occasion a drover sitting in the inglenook had asked Cruikshank what he thought of that other travelling preacher, George Whitfield, and in reply the rogue priest had referred to him as the cross-eyed son of a Gloucester tavern keeper. This was a cheap jibe that brought him a round of raucous laughter from his drunken audience.

Days later, when I was out shooting with my younger brother, Giles, who was at the time studying for the priesthood, I deliberately brought Whitfield into our conversation and his face had lit up at the mention of his name. Although frowned upon by the conservative establishment of the Church, the unconventional priest was something of a hero to Giles and his fellow students at theological college. My little brother confirmed that Whitfield *did* have an unfortunate turn in his eye and his widowed mother *did* run an inn in Gloucester but went on to tell me that his idol had gone to Oxford University, as a servitor at Pembroke College, shining the shoes and carrying the books of the more affluent undergraduates in order to pay for his tuition. It was at

Oxford that he met John and Charles Wesley.

Giles was full of stories about the roving cleric, of the time when, on a visit to Cambuslang in Scotland, no less than thirty thousand people had turned out to hear him, and of another occasion on Hanham Mount, south east of Bristol, a centre of vice in all its worst forms. There, Whitfield had preached to thousands of miners who lived like heathens and his words had caused those rough, tough colliers to weep, their tears coursing in white streaks down their coal-blackened cheeks.

Josh snapped me out of my reverie. 'Whitfield has a very powerful voice,' he said, stuffing his tobacco pouch back in his pocket. 'And an actor's way with him that held his audience spellbound — me included! Some folk actually screamed out loud and fell down on their knees in the mud. When it was all over I fought my way through the crowd to get to him. I felt I just had to tell him my story — and when he said he knew my Emily, and that she was safe and well, I don't mind telling you, Master Thomas, he had me shouting, 'Hallelujah!''

'Get to the orphanage part, Napper!' I said impatiently.

'Yes, yes. Well, apparently, the last time Whitfield was in Charleston, Leila Sculley had sought him out. As bold as brass, she asked him for his help to get Emily away. As the Reverend was on his way south at the time he took the two women with him to this orphanage he'd set up in Savannah. When I spoke to him he'd just come from there and he said that when he left they were both happily working in the kitchen.'

'I thought this Leila Sculley was half-witted?'

'That's what I was led to believe by the servants at the Harwood mansion. A big simpleton is how they described her. The story goes that she was one of Harwood's hostesses until one day she refused to go along with one of his drunken guest's perverted suggestions. Apparently the colonel lost his temper and ordered a couple of his overseers to flog her, and wouldn't let 'em stop 'til she'd passed out. From that day on she kept herself to herself and never spoke to anyone.

'The Reverend said she's a big woman right enough, tall and big boned, and with large hands, but, strangely, he described her as being most self-assured. He even went on to say that my Emily was fortunate to have her as her protector.'

★   ★   ★

The waterfront at Savannah was crowded with people; anxious-looking men arguing loudly with each other and taught-faced women, old before their time, with babies cradled in shawls tightly bound to their breasts and small wide-eyed children clutching firmly to their skirts. There was great excitement as we neared the jetty. Willing hands caught the painter and the boat was tied up almost before the rowers had time to ship the oars.

The two soldiers were eagerly helped ashore. I scrambled up onto the quay and then, reaching down, gave Josh a hand up. By this time Obadiah and the young subaltern were completely surrounded by the townspeople. There was much shaking of hands and backslapping. Those not thus engaged were peering out across the water. Men were hugging their wives and holding up their small children so they could see the soldiers over the heads of the crowd. Everyone looked happy and somehow relieved.

An elderly man stepped forward. By his bearing I judged him to be an old soldier, and from the respect afforded him by the people he was obviously a person of importance in the community.

'Nathaniel Pendleton, gentlemen,' he said, raising his hat. 'From England are you? Don't tell me, your ship's anchored down river and you've been sent on ahead, to arrange billeting, that sort of thing. I know, I've done it myself many times.' He stopped before the young officer, his face grim. 'You have no reason to know it, sir, but you have arrived at a most opportune moment. A French force was landed just south of the Altamaha two days ago and is reported to be moving in this direction. How many men do you have with you, a Company? Go tell your Major there will be no problem with billeting his men. Just tell him to get them ashore as quickly as he can.'

It was Obadiah who answered with a chirpy, 'We're not from England, sir. We're your neighbours, from Carolina.' He drew himself up and smiling proudly, added, 'Colonel Harwood's Militia.'

A brief shadow of disappointment flitted across Pendleton's face but he quickly rallied himself and still addressing Lacoste, he said, 'Never mind. The French believe us to be completely undefended so even finding militiamen here will come as a nasty shock to them. Get 'em ashore, lad, get 'em ashore.'

Lacoste didn't flinch. 'There's just the two of us, sir,' he announced grandly. 'We are here to gain intelligence and report back to Colonel Harwood without delay.'

'Just the two of you!' Pendleton bellowed. His naturally ruddy complexion became even redder and he looked as though he were about to explode. 'By the time you and your pimple-faced friend get back to Charleston the French will be upon us!'

He then glared at my little group. Coggins, standing in the cutter was passing up the muskets to Nolan and Fowler on the quay. 'And if you're here for sport, gentlemen, I suggest you seek your game elsewhere.'

With his hopes of a relieving force dashed, it was understandable that he should be upset. I explained that we were there simply to collect a young woman from the orphanage.

'Then you had best hurry before it's cut off,' he said grumpily.

My first thought was to do just that. Dash off to the orphanage and get Emily out while there was still time. This wasn't my fight, I told myself. What right had I to interfere in the problems of these colonials? But then I looked around at the people here on the jetty, at the frightened women and the worried faces of the men and I knew I couldn't just walk away and leave them to it.

I motioned Lacoste to one side. 'We have to do something to halt the French,' I whispered. 'I suggest we join forces.'

He looked disparagingly at Josh who was

standing by my side. 'Your friend is obviously not a fighting man so that makes us only six in number. You are the senior officer, Major. Are you proposing that the six of us take on what could be as much as two hundred men — and from one of the finest armies in the world?'

'I have every admiration for the French,' I said. 'But you'd be amazed at the amount of havoc a few sharpshooters can wreak amongst even the best trained and disciplined of soldiers.'

His face lit up. 'Skirmishers you mean?'

'Precisely.'

Lacoste was carrying a musket, which, in the British army, was unusual for an officer. 'Are you proficient with that weapon?' I asked.

'I'm pretty slick at loading and shooting, but I can't hold a candle to Obadiah for accuracy. He was shooting squirrels for his daddy when he was just six years old. What about your men, Major, are they sharpshooters?'

'We are all well practiced with the musket but both Nolan and Fowler are snipers.'

He looked at me quizzically. 'Snipers, Major? I'm not familiar with the term.'

'It's my old regiment's word for a marksman who shoots from a hiding place.

71

I'll explain later. But sniping's the only thing we can do in the circumstances.'

'You mean shoot a few of them from the cover of the swamp?'

'Yes, and then move to another location where they're not expecting us to be and do the same again.'

He was really excited now. 'Now you're talking my language, Major. Most folk won't dare venture into the swamp but it's like home to me, it's where I grew up.'

'You'd better pacify these good townsfolk,' I said. 'Tell them we'll send word to Colonel Harwood and in the meantime, we'll do what we can to delay the French.'

6

Having ascertained from Nathaniel Pendleton that the orphanage lay approximately ten miles to the north, I surprised Josh Napper by asking him to remove his hat, which I then proceeded to fill with coins from my money belt.

'Go to the livery stables and hire a carriage,' I told him, 'and while you're there ask them to send word to Colonel Harwood about the invasion. Speed is of the essence. You must get to the orphanage and bring Emily back here before the French block the road . . . Oh, and when you've got her safely back you might check with that shipping agent to see if he's actually booked our trunk on a vessel bound for England.' I still harboured visions of the man pocketing my money and never seeing my belongings again.

Pendleton volunteered to go with him to the stables. It was patently obvious that his purpose was to ensure that the message for the colonel was sent by the fastest means but he put my mind at ease when he said he knew the shipping agent. 'He's a fellow mason, a brother, so you can stop worrying about him, sir, and devote your energies to confusing the French!'

He went on to tell us the invasion party had been seen following the old Cherokee trail and was now less then a day's march from Savannah so, with no further delay, we set off to intercept them. Chambers would have dearly liked to come with us but his orders were to take us to Savannah and then return to the *Caprice*. He bade us goodbye, explaining that even though Jensen may not have found a full cargo yet he could well be in need of his bo'sun. I waved him off feeling I was right about a bit of responsibility bringing out the best in a man.

We passed a number of abandoned homesteads on the way south, their occupants having fled to the comparative safety of the town. Coggins and Fowler did a smart right wheel into of one of them, the little Cockney immediately reappearing with a large slice of pie. He justified his action by saying it had been left lying on the kitchen table so it would only go mouldy or be eaten by rats, which I suppose was true. Coggins however, couldn't use the same argument for the flask of wine he was swigging.

Lacoste insisted we left a signed note promising to pay for what had been taken, and to this I agreed.

By late afternoon Coggins was complaining of the heat. It was vital to my plan that we meet the French while they were still on the track through the marshland but I could see that a combination of alcohol and humidity was having an adverse affect on the big man so I called a halt to enable him to cool down.

Perspiration was streaming down his face, his shirt was wet through, and the strong smell that emanated from his body only the mosquitoes found attractive. As soon as we stopped the voracious insects swarmed around him and the sound of the tormented man repeatedly slapping his exposed flesh was pitiful to hear.

'After your long service in India I'm surprised the heat bothers you so much,' I said irritably.

'The heat's different here, Major,' he gasped. 'It was hot in India right enough, but it was dry there. I could cope with that. Here it's sort of damp, like one o' them Turkish steam rooms.'

'And why is it that mosquitoes seem to bother you more than the rest of us?' I added. It was a ridiculous thing to say but his incessant slapping and cursing was getting on my nerves.

Fowler butted in, a toothy grin spread across his narrow face. 'It's all that rum in his blood, Major,' he quipped. 'The little blighters can't get enough of it.'

It wasn't long before Coggins said he would rather sweat than be eaten alive and begged to be on the move once more.

When we set off again the young ensign positioned himself at my side.

'How do you plan to use our six muskets to the best effect, Major?' he asked eagerly.

My mind was still on Coggins and the mosquitoes, and without thinking, I said, 'By only having three men fire them.'

Seeing his jaw drop, I quickly went on to explain. 'Here's my strategy, Mr Lacoste. You and I, together with the mosquitoes' friend, Daniel Coggins here, are to be loaders. Fowler, Obadiah and Nolan are the shooters. As soon as we get sight or sound of the French we will deploy into the swamp. There, I shall rely on your familiarity with the terrain to find a hidden path that will keep us no more that fifty yards from the enemy. When we draw level with the head of their column, we keep going but the shooters will stand fast, count to thirty slowly and then fire. Meanwhile, Coggins and me will be following you through the swamp, keeping parallel with the column to a likely spot a few yards further on. There, we will stop and wait for the shooters to catch up with us. When they do they will swap their spent muskets for our loaded ones. We leave them there and go to a new position where we reload and wait for the shooters, and so on.'

Lacoste could hardly contain his enthusiasm. 'What about your men, Major?' he asked excitedly. 'They're good enough shots are they?'

'Don't you worry about them. As I've told you, they're snipers.'

He looked at me enquiringly and I held up my hands in mock surrender. 'I'm sorry, I know I promised to explain that term to you. I had to do the same when I arrived in India but by the time I left, the expression was in everyday use by the Company's soldiers.'

Up ahead, Fowler began to whistle *The British Grenadiers*, Coggins took it up and, consciously or not, one by one, we all fell into step.

'A snipe is a wading bird,' I told him, 'with a long, straight bill that he uses for digging in the mud for his food. They live on the swampy edges of our meres in Cheshire and are quite a table delicacy, tasting rather like duck. Like other wildfowl, they are shot from cover but they are possibly the hardest of all small game birds to hit as they fly in an undulating, weaving pattern at remarkably high speed. The men who shoot them are called 'snipers' and are regarded as being outstanding marksmen . . . It was a practice in my regiment for the officers to organise snipe shooting parties.'

'And how did you do, sir?' he asked with a grin.

'Let me say I enjoyed the open air luncheon rather more than the shooting.'

Suddenly, up ahead, Coggins hissed a warning. 'Shut up Archie and listen.'

We all strained our ears. Yes, then I heard it too. Those arrogant Frenchies were marching to drum and fife!

'Right, everyone,' I hissed. 'We now follow Ensign Lacoste into the swamp.'

There was a general murmur of agreement.

'Which side of the track do you favour, Mr Lacoste?'

'The right side is drier and shouldn't be too difficult to get through,' he whispered. 'The left looks downright inhospitable. It's probably full of alligators and it'll be alive with mosquitoes — that's the way we go.'

Coggins groaned.

Once in the cover of the swamp, we stopped and loaded our muskets. I suggested that the militiamen reverse their red coats so that the less obvious brown lining would be on the outside. Lacoste saw the wisdom in this, immediately taking off his coat and ordering Obadiah to do the same.

As this was where we would leave the three shooters, I shook the hand of each of them in turn. When I got to Fowler, I whispered, 'Remember the tactics on the ship. Shoot anyone giving orders. Tell the others.'

'Right you are, Major. Good luck.'

The moustachioed French soldiers made a colourful sight in their collarless off-white coats with blue cuffs, matching blue waist-coats and tricorns trimmed with silver lace. Because of the narrowness of the track they marched in a column of twos, but smartly, and led by a small drum corps and two standard bearers. I thanked my lucky stars, for this was just a platoon, or section, as the French call a group of no more than fifty infantrymen. Their commanding officer, a lieutenant mounted on a rather fine horse, preceded them, his silver buttons glinting in the sunlight.

It wasn't long before the first shots rang out. The lieutenant was jerked out of his saddle and the two ensigns fell backwards into the leading musicians, their flags fluttering down and draping over their bodies almost symbolically.

Orders were shouted and the French soldiers, with their muskets now ported defensively, stood peering nervously into the swamp. Nolan, Fowler and Obadiah slid into the small clearing where we were waiting. Weapons were quickly exchanged and with Lacoste leading, we loaders waded out to a small muddy island that was opposite the rear of the column. I was just tamping down the wadding in the musket I was loading when there was another crackle of shots and three more Frenchmen fell. The shooters arrived wet and breathless, weapons were swapped and we made off again, this time returning to our original position opposite the head of the column. There was now some sporadic fire coming from the French and a few musket balls ripped through the moss that draped the trees. Some of the more courageous among them advanced into the swamp. They were the next targets. We traded muskets again and splashed our way to a new hide. The French began arguing among themselves.

'One more volley should do it,' Lacoste whispered.

It did; the bulk of the soldiers began retreating back the way they had come, while the more vociferous among those that remained remonstrated with the deserters, urging them to stand fast. The next shots silenced them.

We didn't need to do any more shooting. Lacoste led us deep into the swamp where we stayed for about an hour, smoking our pipes to deter the mosquitoes. When we got back to the track there was no sign of the French. They had taken their colours but left their dead lying where they had fallen. The lieutenant's mount was grazing not far away. Nolan, displaying the natural affinity the Irish seem to have with horses, went over and spoke to it quietly. It nuzzled into his shoulder.

Two of the dead were pioneers with small shovels attached to their backpacks. These I gave to Coggins and Fowler with orders to dig two pits, deep enough to protect the bodies from scavenging animals, one for the officer and a larger one as a communal grave for the other ranks. I gave Nolan the task of going through the dead men's pockets to find some form of identification. I intended to mark the graves and take a list of those interred back to Savannah. These were brave men and I felt their last resting place should be recorded. Ironically, it had been the brave men who had died this day and the cowards allowed to run away, but that was often the way of things on the battlefield.

It was dusk now and the evening air was cooler. Coggins stripped off his shirt and with the soil being soft, the two men soon had the pits dug. Nolan managed to find something on each of the dead soldiers to identify them so I was able to write my list. Then Nolan and I laid the French officer in the smaller trench and helped Coggins and Fowler to carry the rest of the bodies to the larger one. With Coggins waiting impatiently to fill them in, Fowler and I stood in silence while Nolan recited the prayer for eternal rest known to every good Catholic.

It was while we were standing respectfully to attention that it occurred to me that the two militiamen had been missing throughout this morbid task.

Archie Fowler had found a hunting knife on the body of the French lieutenant and he chose this occasion to solemnly present it to me. 'The lads thought you should have this, Major,' he said. 'A sort of souvenir.'

I took it out of its leather sheath and weighed it in my hand. It was a businesslike weapon but well balanced. I'd never seen anything quite like it. The foot-long blade was a quarter of an inch thick at the grip and two inches across at its widest part. But for the guard and its sharp, tapering point it was more like a kitchen knife than a dagger. 'Probably Walloon, made in Belgium,' I said, thinking aloud.

'Nah! Made in Birmingham more like! Obie says you can buy any amount of 'em up north. The Hudson's Bay Company ships 'em over from England for the fur trappers.'

I ran my thumb across its edge. It was so sharp I could have shaved with it. Instead I used it to cut down some branches to fashion into markers for the graves.

It was fast growing dark, so while I was hacking away at the trees I decided to build a bivouac and make camp for the night. I told Nolan and Coggins to make similar shelters and set Fowler to work gathering wood for a fire, which was blazing nicely by the time Obadiah and Lacoste returned. As they were each carrying a brace of rabbits I was inclined to forgive them for their absence.

'We also filled our canteens,' the ensign said. 'It's fresh water from a spring but I recommend you boil it. I've still got some coffee left, or would you Englishmen prefer tea?'

Nolan drew attention to the inaccuracy of this generalisation by noisily clearing his throat.

It had been a long, hard day and having dined like kings on roast rabbit and coffee, and in spite of the ceaseless cacophony emanating from the myriad of creatures that inhabited the swamp, we all slept soundly and awoke refreshed and ready for the trek back to Savannah.

It was late afternoon by the time we reached the town. Dogs barked at us and a few bold youngsters ventured out to see who it was on the road. When we got to the waterfront we found quite a reception committee waiting for us. I looked for Josh but I couldn't see him. Nathaniel Pendleton was there however, right in the forefront.

There was a small cheer and some ragged clapping as he stepped forward.

'We heard the shooting. The fact that you're here and the French aren't must mean you've succeeded,' he said. 'I can't begin to thank you.'

There was some more clapping and I held up my hand. 'We've bought you some time, sir, that's all,' I said. 'The French troops we encountered have retreated but they could well return with new commanders, officers from their ship perhaps — and furthermore, I'm not sure if the soldiers we saw was the entire expeditionary force.'

We must have looked a scruffy lot. The militiamen had turned their coats back the right way so that the relatively clean red material was again on the outside but, like the rest of us, their faces were dirty and their gaiters were stiff with mud. We were all desperately in need of a good wash and a shave, and to top it all, Coggins' scarred and pockmarked face, not pretty at the best of times, was now covered in lumps from the mosquito bites.

'You have done quite enough,' Pendleton said. 'I can only thank God you have all come back.' He looked beyond me to where Nolan was standing with the horse. 'In fact there seems to be one extra in your party.'

All the way back I'd been racking my brains what to do with the horse and now the answer came to me in a flash. 'It belonged to the French officer,' I said. 'Could it be sold and the proceeds given to the orphanage perhaps?'

'Certainly, an excellent idea . . . I've sent gallopers to Colonel Harwood and to the Highlanders explaining our situation. I confidently expect to hear back today that one or both are on their way to defend our border.'

He was still talking to me but I really wasn't listening. I was busily scanning the crowd hoping to see some sign of Josh — and suddenly, there he was! I could just make out the wide-brimmed hat bobbing up occasionally above the ranks of townspeople as he forced his way through them. Completely forgetting the old gentleman, I went forward to meet him. He looked hot and bothered — and, damn it, he was on his own!

'Napper!' I yelled at him. 'Have you been to the orphanage? Where the devil is Emily?'

'You might well ask, Master Thomas,' he growled. 'Yes, I've been to the orphanage all right but Emily weren't there. This Leila Sculley has taken it upon herself to get Emily back to England.' He drove a fist into the palm of his hand. 'Oh, she means well I suppose, and they weren't to know we were on our way to fetch 'em were they? Apparently they talked a carter into giving 'em a lift to Charleston. So while we was sailing round here on the *Avenger's* cutter, they was going across country in the opposite direction.'

That was possibly the last thing I wanted to hear. But I'd be damned if I'd travelled over four thousand miles and got this close to Emily only to lose her again. We had to get back to Charleston, and as quickly as possible.

'I told you to hire a wagon to fetch Emily from the orphanage,' I demanded. 'Do you still have it?'

Josh cast his eyes to the ground. 'Well, actually I bought one,' he mumbled, adding defensively, 'You did give me rather a lot of money, Master Thomas, and that man there,' he said, pointing at Pendleton, 'said it would work out cheaper to buy one and sell it once we was done with it.'

'Good!' I said, which surprised him. 'A big one is it?'

'It is that, sir, with a pair of fine horses.'

'Excellent. It couldn't be better. I suggest we waste no more time. It will be cooler travelling now so let's collect our things from the Marine Tavern and get on the road.'

I went back to Pendleton and apologised for my rudeness. Handing him the lists of names, I told him about the graves out on the Cherokee trail.

'You'll find them marked with a couple of simple crosses — just branches lashed together, you understand. We did say some words over them but your priest here may want to do the job properly . . . Oh, and I'm afraid the orphanage will have to do without the proceeds from the sale of horse for a while. I'll need it to get me to Charleston.'

7

After a quick wash and a change of linen we were on our way.

The wagon Josh had bought was a large, covered, four-wheeler drawn by two powerful-looking horses. Lacoste, our self-appointed guide for the journey, rode with him, up on the box, Nolan and Coggins sat inside on the luggage while Fowler and Obadiah chose to walk alongside the heavy vehicle as it bumped and swayed along the pot-holed trail.

I rode on ahead on the French officer's horse, keeping my eye open for the stone cairns built to resemble human figures that Lacoste had told me were the natives' trail markers.

It was good to feel a horse between my knees again. It was like being back home; the only thing missing, of course, was my dog, Hagar, running alongside me. Hagar is a lurcher, a poacher's dog, bred by Irish Gypsies for speed and sharp eyesight. There's both greyhound and collie in Hagar. I'd found her wandering the lanes near my family home in Cheshire. She was thin, half-starved and pining for her owner, who was probably doing penance for his crime in some lock-up somewhere. Regular meals and lots of exercise soon had her back on form and she now earns her keep working for Finch, catching rats in the stables, but when I'm home I'm pleased to say she chooses to be with me.

It was much easier travelling in the cool of the evening and in spite of having to negotiate the occasional fallen tree and stop to lever one of the wheels out of a bog, we made good time. When it became too dark to travel in safety we made camp. We lit a fire to cook the food we had brought with us and posted a piquet just in case a native or a runaway slave should take a fancy to the horses. I had just rolled myself up in my blanket to get some sleep when I heard one of our sentries shout the familiar challenge, 'Halt! Who goes there?' The deep, gruff voice was that of Daniel Coggins who, together with Fowler, had volunteered to take the first watch.

'Friend,' came the reply. 'Sergeant Bennett, Harwood's Militia, and two men.'

Coggins, who was never one for correct military protocol, growled, 'Come closer, so's I can see you.'

Lacoste scrambled out from under the wagon. 'I know Sergeant Bennett, sentry,' he called out.

Throwing off my blanket, I grabbed my sword and followed him.

Coggins was standing on the far side of the campfire with his musket trained on the visitors, now clearly identifiable as red-coated soldiers. I caught sight of Fowler's weapon pointing out of the shadows a few paces behind the group.

On seeing the young ensign, the sergeant snapped smartly to attention and saluted. 'Mr Lacoste, sir,' he said, somewhat surprised. 'We're camped back along the trail, sir, the full company, on our way to Savannah. We saw the glow of your fire and the major sent me to find out who you were.'

I told Coggins to stand at ease. The big man lowered his musket and out of the corner of my eye I saw Fowler do the same.

'I'll come back with you, sergeant,' Lacoste said. 'I'm on my way to report to Colonel Harwood anyway. He'll no doubt want me to join the column.'

The sergeant's face remained impassive, his eyes looking straight ahead. 'The colonel isn't with us, sir. Major Reid is the officer in charge.'

Now why did that not surprise me? It was typical of that overdressed dandy to find some pressing commitment to prevent him from being where he should be, leading his men into battle. 'Tell me, Mr Lacoste,' I said, 'has the militia seen action before?'

The ensign drew himself up. 'Indeed we have, sir. We have successfully defended the colony against attacks by pirates and hostile natives on a number of occasions.'

'But this the first time you've had to face trained and experienced soldiers, yes?'

Lacoste was quick to grasp my meaning. 'And we have Major Reid, the schoolmaster, in command,' he said, ruefully shaking his head. 'To him a battlefield is a chessboard with the two armies drawn up facing each other in neatly dressed-off ranks. He wouldn't dream of doing what we did in the swamp, what do you call it, sniping? You must come with me, Major, and tell him battles are not won by carefully rehearsed set pieces.'

I agreed to accompany him to the militia's camp and pay my compliments to Major Reid. I said I'd also give him the benefit of my advice, should he ask for it, but only on the understanding that it would not delay my journey to Charleston.

This seemed to satisfy him and he rushed off shouting to Obadiah to get their things together.

The militia's camp was only a short distance away. It lay in a depression behind a stand of trees, which is why we hadn't seen their campfires.

On our way there, Lacoste prepared me for my meeting with Major Reid. He described him as a man who lived in awe of Colonel Harwood. 'It's the colonel's lifestyle, you understand,' he said. 'The plantation, the slaves, the big house in town — and coming from a noble family! Samuel Reid comes from humble stock. Not that there's any shame in that, but he never knew his father, and his mother scrubbed floors and took in washing to feed him. It was the local priest who recognised young Samuel's potential and paid for his education. The major eventually became our local schoolmaster, and as such, he is a man of some standing in the community . . . And because he's a man of letters, the colonel is quite happy to leave it up to him to read up on military tactics and familiarise himself with all the laid down drills. The major's a grand man on the parade ground.'

'What will happen when you came face to face with the French?'

Lacoste looked beyond me and into the distance. 'The militia will fight bravely, Major,' he said.

The young ensign took me along to Major Reid's tent while Obadiah went off to brag to his mates about recent events.

We found the expedition's senior officer

sitting at a folding table busily studying a large map, a bottle and glass by his hand. He looked what he was, a schoolmaster, a thin, bookish man with rounded shoulders and a drooping moustache. He also looked worried.

I was introduced as Major Neville of the twenty-second.

'The twenty-second? Whose regiment is that?' he said absently.

'It's the county regiment of Cheshire, Major,' I replied. 'The Colonel of the Regiment is Reuben Neville.'

He went back to studying his map. 'Who's he, your father?' he said disinterestedly.

I didn't bother to explain that Reuben Neville was my uncle or that I had recently resigned my commission, but asked instead why Colonel Harwood was not on this expedition.

There was a long pause before Reid mumbled, 'The colonel, er, wasn't able to come.'

Lacoste pounced on this. 'With respect, sir,' he said, 'what do you mean, 'wasn't able to come'? Is Colonel Harwood ill?'

'Colonel Harwood is recovering from a head injury,' he replied without looking up.

Turning to me, Lacoste said gravely, 'It must be serious to prevent the colonel from being here,' and I wondered whom he was trying to convince, himself or me?

I asked Reid if Harwood had been involved in an accident and I was shocked when the major leaned back in his chair, looked at me with tired eyes and said, 'A harlot hit him with a piss pot!'

Lacoste gasped and it was all I could do to stop myself laughing out loud.

'Only the officers know,' Reid said wearily, pouring himself a drink, which I guessed wasn't his first. He didn't offer us one but under the circumstances perhaps he could be forgiven for this lapse of good manners.

There followed an uncomfortable moment when no one spoke. Major Reid swallowed his drink, grimacing as the raw spirit hit the back of his throat.

'The servants found him,' he croaked, pausing for a moment to allow his gullet time to recover before continuing in his normal voice. 'He was lying naked on his bed. He'd been, er, entertaining a lady, that much the servants knew. She had arrived after dark and she was long gone by the time someone thought to see why he hadn't appeared for breakfast. The footman who let her in described her as a big, good-looking woman with piercing eyes that seemed to look right through you.'

I immediately thought of Leila Sculley.

Harwood was vain and conceited enough to believe Leila would want him to make love to her even though he was responsible for having her beaten senseless. It was a forlorn hope but I asked if it could possibly have been an accident.

'No chance,' Reid replied. 'He'd been bashed on the head with the chamber pot. The surgeon said that if it hadn't been for the unusual thickness of his skull he would be a dead man.'

'And the motive?'

'Clearly robbery. A small leather bag was taken that contained a sizeable amount of money which the colonel said he'd won at the tables.'

I couldn't in all honesty say I was saddened by the news. After what he did to my Emily, to Leila Sculley and to goodness knows how many other vulnerable women, I felt the man had received his just deserts. In fact, I couldn't wait to tell Josh.

Reid meticulously plotted the position of our encounter with the French on his map and listened carefully to my thoughts on the enemy's possible next move, scratching notes in the margin of the map with his pen as I spoke.

I left him just as morose and worried-looking as I'd found him, whereas I, on the other hand, arrived back at camp in exceedingly good humour.

The early light of dawn was filling the sky, the air was fresh and invigorating and in whatever part of the world I may find myself, the birds' morning chorus never fails to raise my spirits.

I found Nolan on sentry duty. I kicked some life into the fire and told him to put some water on for tea while I roused the others.

Unlike Major Reid, I don't believe in keeping things from my men so I wasted no time in telling them that Colonel Harwood had been put out of action by a blow to the head.

Fowler scrambled out of his blanket and proceeded to shake it vigorously to rid it of the bugs that had crawled in to share the warmth of his body during the night. 'Well, that's a turn up and no mistake,' he said, and winked at Coggins who was similarly engaged, adding, 'What happened, sir, didn't the colonel duck quick enough this time?' They both laughed heartily at this.

The news brought a big smile to Josh's round face. 'How is he, Master Thomas?' he asked eagerly. 'I hope he's got a nasty headache.'

'He was unconscious when the militia marched out,' I said, and left it at that.

The men of Harwood's Militia were still breaking camp as we rode past. I felt a little apprehensive to be setting off into unknown territory without a guide but the trail had been well used and had the Indian signs not been there I still wouldn't have wandered off it. It was deeply rutted in places by wagon wheels and had been well trampled by the hooves of many animals, reminding me of the drover's trails through my home county back in England.

The way ahead was clear but with the heavy wagon only moving at walking pace our progress was painfully slow. Eventually my horse got fed up with having to keep standing still to wait for the others to catch up so, leaving Nolan, the only former NCO, in charge of the party, I rode off alone for Charleston harbour.

The French officer's mount was a fine animal. I set off at a canter but when we came to a flattish grassy plain I gave him his head and he covered the ground like a racehorse, enjoying every moment. I was sorry to have to rein him in when the going ahead appeared doubtful but the last thing I wanted was a hoof going down a gopher hole. I made good time however, arriving at the harbour in the early hours of the following morning.

The water was full of small boats but there were two ocean-going ships moored in the deep-water channel, one looking very much like the *Caprice*. I hoped this meant Emily and her companion were still there, waiting to sail back to England with Captain Jensen.

I found a livery stable for my horse and then went in search of Alistair Mackay.

The little harbourmaster wasn't hard to find. In fact it was he who saw me first. 'Major!' he shouted excitedly, and leaving the group of longshoremen he had been talking to, he came hurrying across the jetty towards me. 'The messenger from Savannah said the French had crossed the Altamaha and the Highlanders were not there to deal with them.' He looked at me quizzically. 'He said you and your men had gone to stop them.'

I smiled. 'We did, and now your militia are on their way to make sure they stay stopped. I met them on the way here.'

'You're an amazing man, Major Neville,' he said, gazing at me with undisguised admiration that I found rather embarrassing and I was relieved when he changed the subject with, 'So you heard the news about Colonel Harwood?'

'Yes, Major Reid told me. He said he'd been robbed.'

'What d'you make of it, Major?'

Leila Sculley is what I made of it. From the footman's description it could well have been his former gaming party hostess exacting revenge for the savage beating he had given her. Could she have also taken the money-bag?

I dragged my thoughts back to the matter in hand and completely disregarding his question, I asked him to confirm that one of the ships was in fact the *Caprice*, adding urgently, 'Would you know if Jensen has two lady passengers for England?'

'Aye, you're quite right about that being Captain Jensen's ship. He's on board now waiting for some indigo to complete his cargo and then he's away. He doesn't have any passengers to my knowledge but I ken two ladies looking for a ship to take them to England.'

I felt like hugging the little man. 'Do you know where they are now?' I asked excitedly.

'Indeed I do, laddie,' he said with a grin. 'They're bound for New York and then Liverpool. I fixed them up with the passage myself — on a schooner out of Bermuda that put in here to drop off a few barrels of molasses.'

My warm feeling for the harbourmaster was cooling rapidly.

'The wee lassie said it was perfect,' Mackay continued. 'Apparently Liverpool was the very port she wanted to go to, much nearer her village than London she said. It had an unusual name, her village.' He snapped his fingers trying to remember.

'Goostrey,' I suggested.

'Aye, that's it, Goose-tree. The schooner's master was reluctant to take them at first. Sailors are a superstitious lot, y'ken. He kept going on about it being unlucky to take women passengers, but the glint of the big woman's gold coins soon changed his mind, I can tell ye!'

So, Leila Sculley did take Harwood's money!

'When did the schooner sail?' I asked.

Mackay rubbed his chin. 'That'll be a week last Tuesday. Aye, that's when it was. All of ten days ago now, laddie,' he said.

Damnation! I took several deep breaths to calm myself down, reminding myself that Emily didn't even know her father was in the colonies looking for her, let alone me. But I had come so close! And now the gap between us was widening again.

Desperately, I asked, 'Do you have someone who could to row me out to the *Caprice* — now?'

8

Captain Jensen was delighted to see me. The news of my encounter with the French expedition had reached him and he was eager to know all the details. He guessed correctly that I'd come to see him about a passage back to London and was genuinely saddened when I told him that Emily would not be in my party.

'The indigo I wait for is here, Major. When is loaded we go. *Caprice* is fast ship and we save two weeks sailing eastwards. You soon be with your Emily.'

'Why should it take less time to sail home to England than it does to get here?' I asked. It was a typical landlubber's question. Six months as a reluctant deckhand in His Majesty's Navy hardly qualified me as a navigator.

'We leave London for the Americas we go due west, right?' He waited for me to reply. It seemed logical to me so I agreed. 'Wrong!' he said. 'If we sail due west we sail into wind and square-rigger cannot tack upwind. So we go southwest to Azores. Find wind there to West Indies. This is route of Columbus, yes?'

'Yes,' I said, feeling like the schoolroom dunce.

'From Gulf of Florida we sail in strong current northwards along coast of America.'

Jensen stood looking at me to see if I had taken this in, and satisfied that I had, he carried on. 'Now, *leaving* Americas, this current is like great river in the ocean, hundreds of miles wide. It takes us north along coast, then northeast to Iceland, England, and to my country, Norway. So journey is shorter and quicker.'

'Is this current always there?'

'Yes. Spanish sailed it eastwards for many years but keeping knowledge secret. Nantucket whalers too have used it for years but it was not on any charts until recently . . . Now, there are now five of you, yes?' I nodded. 'Good. I put you in two-berth cabin again and others will have four-berth — yes — unless you want Emily's father share with you?'

'Josh Napper may dress like a gentleman, Captain, but he's one of my father's tenants,' I retorted quickly, too quickly perhaps.

Jensen looked puzzled. 'But his daughter — she is your sweetheart, no?'

He was right, of course. If Josh wasn't of my class, then neither was his daughter. I swiftly changed the subject to the question of payment. 'I can give you a note here and now,' I said, 'that you can present at my bank in London, or I can pay the Blooms when we dock.'

He thrust his bearded chin forward defiantly and said, 'I not accept money from men who risk life saving my ship from pirates.'

I argued that Josh had taken no part in the sea battle and I should at least pay for the food my party would consume during the coming weeks.

Raising his hands in mock surrender, he said, 'All right, Major, I make note in log that you volunteer to pay for victuals and one passenger.' He smiled and shook his handsome leonine head, adding, 'I leave you to tell Blooms when we reach London.'

Mackay's boatman rowed me back to the pier where I found the harbourmaster talking to Barney Nolan.

On seeing me, my valet, forever the soldier, put his heels together and squared his shoulders. 'The others are at the end of the jetty with the wagon awaiting your orders, Major,' he reported. Then, relaxing a little, he added with a smile, 'This gentleman was telling me you've been arranging passage for us back to England on the *Caprice*.'

'It's all settled, Nolan. Now, double away

and tell Napper to bring the wagon down here.'

Nolan left, whistling through his fingers and waving his arms. This was no doubt a pre-arranged signal to Josh who was sitting in the wagon, and it wasn't long before the big, heavy vehicle was rumbling along the jetty with Fowler and Coggins walking beside it.

This got me thinking about the wagon and its horses, plus the French officer's horse that I'd left in the livery stable. I asked the harbourmaster if he would help me dispose of them.

He signalled for me to wait and shouted to the Irishman's rapidly retreating figure, 'Leave anything not wanted on voyage down there, Mr Nolan. Where that lighter's berthed. Tell the loaders I said its to go as *Caprice's* cargo. Then bring the cabin baggage up here.'

He then turned back to me. 'Sorry about that,' he said. 'Now I'd like to help ye laddie. Good horses are always in demand, and it shouldn't be too difficult to find somebody to buy the wagon, but as you can see, the indigo that Captain Jensen's been waiting for is being loaded on a lighter at this very moment. Folk hereabouts are tough bargainers. Once they get a sniff you're in a hurry to sell ye'll no get a good price.'

I didn't need to stop and think. 'Can I leave it with you to get the best price you can?' I pleaded. 'And then send the money to the Bethesda Orphanage near Savannah?'

Mackay smiled. 'Aye, I'll do that with pleasure, laddie. The Reverend Whitfield is a good man — and a good Calvinist. Leave it to me, I'll see to it.'

He looked round for the boatman and found him sitting on an abandoned cask, filling his pipe. 'Collins,' he called. 'I'll need you to take Major Neville and four men, plus their baggage, out to the *Caprice*.' The man mumbled something about having to make more than one journey to which Mackay replied, 'Then ye'll just have to do that, won't ye?'

9

I spent many a sunny afternoon as a boy in a small boat that Finch, our head groom — and my unofficial tutor in all things a young man should know — had acquired from somewhere. It never occurred to me to ask him where or how it was that a former cavalry sergeant should know how to sail. He and I would go out on Dunmere, the big lake that gave the family home its name, either fishing for the carp that one of my forebears had thoughtfully introduced into its waters, or wildfowling in its reed banks. And until I was forcibly 'pressed' into service in His Britannic Majesty's navy, sailing with Sergeant Finch in our little boat had been the full extent of my nautical experience.

I grant the sea is beautiful but, in my opinion, it is best viewed from the shore, and my short time before the mast did nothing to change that. Ports and docksides are dens of vice and crime. They are sleazy, smelly places, and the ships that use them are not much better. The quarters are cramped, the food gets progressively more inedible and, unless you are sailing in the tropics, there is no escape from the misery of being permanently cold and wet. Mercifully I am not subject to the scourge of seasickness but I still view sailing the ocean as a necessary evil. It is something that, living on an island, can't be avoided if one's need is to travel to other countries; but the least amount of time I spend doing it the better.

For this reason I was grateful to Captain Jensen. The big Norwegian was true to his word, as once we were at sea he crowded on every possible inch of canvas and had the *Caprice* cutting through the water at a speed I had never experienced before, or even thought possible for a ship of her size.

The voyage was uneventful and, for me, boring. At least when I was a deckhand I was kept so busy that one exhausting day blurred into another but as a passenger there is nothing but nothing to do. Conversation soon becomes little more than a passing reference to the weather, and you find yourself walking the deck, day in and day out, just gazing at the waves. To preserve my sanity I would remind myself that each day that passed brought me that much closer to Emily.

The crew though, remained in high spirits throughout the voyage; they were sailing home and they worked with a will. Chambers, their new bo'sun, carried a rope's end, but with him it was more a badge of office than a means of inducement. In fact, more often than not he would get the job in hand done by leading the men in a shanty — himself being the chanter, or 'shanty-man' — the one who sings out the call, to which the sailors bellow out the response.

Chambers had composed a shanty in my honour and he had an annoying habit of using it in preference to any other whenever he saw me on deck.

'Neville is a soldier.'

'*Way, hey, ya!*'

'A soldier and a hero.'

'*Way, hey, ya!*'

There was more but I never heard it, as by the time the hauling party had reached the second '*Way, hey, ya!*' I had dived for cover.

After weeks of looking at nothing but water, eventually the blessed day finally came when the lookout shouted, 'Land ho!'

'Where away?' Captain Jensen yelled.

'Two points off the starboard bow!' came the reply.

He peered through his spyglass and then, with a broad grin on his handsome face, he handed it to me. 'Look, Major. There is Ushant!' He slapped me on the back as if it was I who had skilfully navigated across thousands of miles of ocean to this tiny island just off the north-westernmost tip of France. 'Soon we are in your English Channel, *ja?*'

To finally be in sight of the English coast was heart-warming but I found sailing in the Channel more wearisome than being in mid-Atlantic. More frustration was to follow.

Off Gravesend we hove-to to allow the Trinity House cutter to come alongside and once the pilot was on board we turned westward into the Thames. The tide was in our favour and as we progressed up river, the flat and featureless land on either side gradually gave way to woodland, above which, eventually, the many spires of London could be seen. At this point the river became progressively busier until, arriving at the Pool of London itself, we found it so congested that at some wharves, ships were tied up five and six abreast. I commented on this to the pilot, a craggy-faced seaman from the Isle of Grain.

'There are urchins that scavenge in the mud of the river at low tide, Guv'nor,' he said. 'Mudlarks they call 'em. They claim they can cross the river without getting their feet wet by jumping from boat to boat — and I believe 'em.'

Well, the Mudlarks were out of luck this day as there was a channel between the ships that was wide enough to manoeuvre the

Caprice right up to Bloom's wharf. But there we were forced to tie up alongside a two-masted coaster, that was itself moored to another vessel currently unloading its cargo there. Jensen vaulted over the ship's rail and made his way across the decks of the other craft to the shore. He wasn't gone long but when he returned the look on his face said it all.

'When these ships have offloaded they have to take on new cargo. There's no room at the wharf for lighters to work and old Isaac won't hear of us landing our cargo elsewhere because the river thieves will steal it, so we wait.'

'For how long?' I asked.

'Could be days.'

Nolan was standing not far way. I called him over and told him to get our party assembled on the quarterdeck for an emergency meeting.

Josh was the first to arrive, closely followed by Fowler and Coggins. 'Are we goin' ashore, Major?' the little Cockney asked with a grin.

'As a matter of fact you and Coggins are not,' I told him. 'Well, not for a while. This ship won't be in a position to be unloaded for days so I'm leaving you both here to wait until it is. When our trunk is brought ashore you will collect it and follow us, right?'

110

As I was speaking, the expression on his little ferret-like face changed from eager anticipation to one of disbelief. 'You mean Dan an' me 'ave got to stay on this bleedin' boat twiddlin' our bleedin' thumbs?'

'Of course not. Think of the ship as your townhouse. Go ashore as often as you like, enjoy yourselves . . . Just don't bring any doxies on board — and be sure you're both sober when our trunk is put ashore.'

'What do we do with it then?' he asked cautiously.

Although the London to Manchester stagecoach went under the flamboyant name of the 'Manchester Flyer', such vehicles were heavy and cumbersome so, not relishing the prospect of spending over a week lurching along rutted roads cooped up with a half-dozen strangers, I had already made up my mind to take a leaf out of Josh's book. I would buy a fast chaise for our journey to Cheshire and sell it when we got there.

The trunk was far too big to be carried on anything other than a cart so I decided it was only fair that Fowler should be allowed to employ a similar strategy. Shaking the remaining coins out of my purse, I handed them to him.

'Buy a wagon with a good, strong horse,' I instructed. 'Collect the trunk when it's unloaded and drive it north to Josh Napper's tavern in Goostrey. You've been there before so you know where it is . . . There should be plenty of money left over to pay for decent lodgings on the way — if you don't spend it all on ale!'

That put the smile back on his face.

'Now, I want you to make the best possible speed,' I continued. 'Don't let other carters talk you into waiting around to travel in a group for protection. There isn't a highway-man living that's a match for you and Coggins — but they don't know that so keep your eyes open.'

There was a commotion at the far end of the deck. Someone had come aboard bringing with him a retinue of attendants. When they got nearer I recognised the stooping bird-like figure of old Isaac Bloom. He stopped a pace away from me and stood with eyes downcast. He looked as though he had something important to say but didn't know where or how to begin. Perhaps seeing me again had brought back the moment he was informed of tragic death of his nephew.

I thought it might help if I went first. 'How nice to see you again Mr Bloom,' I said cheerfully.

'I fear I am the bearer of bad news,' he intoned.

My first thought was of the *Avenger*. 'Don't tell me the pirate ship sank like a stone at the auction?' I quipped, forcing a smile to make him feel easier.

He waved a bony hand. 'No, no,' he said dismissively. 'The auction hasn't been held yet. My news concerns your father . . . I am so very sorry to have to tell you he's dead.'

10

Isaac Bloom recommended a carriage maker who had a workshop not far from his offices so, taking Josh and Nolan with me I went to see what he had to offer. From what I saw, I judged the man's workmanship to be excellent but his stock was somewhat limited, having only two chaises for sale, a one-horse two-wheeler and a two-horse four-wheeler. The two-wheeler was too small for our purpose so it had to be the four-wheeler.

A matched pair of horses was acquired and harnessed to the newly acquired vehicle and we set off on our journey northwards.

I assigned Barney Nolan to the rear seat where he now lay slumped morosely, his feet resting on top of the luggage. A relationship of mutual understanding and trust had developed between the Irishman and my father. Nolan's 'da' had been an alcoholic so he was familiar with the sickness and was proud of the part he had played in my father's journey back to sobriety.

Josh was sitting high up on the front seat. Although he was visibly upset when I gave him the news of my father's death, he had insisted on driving the carriage.

I sat beside him wrapped in my own thoughts. How was my mother coping with the loss? Would my father's death undo all the good that had been done to restore her to health after her ordeal at the hands of that damned Edwin Cruikshank? Thank God my uncle, my father's brother, Colonel Reuben Neville, had agreed to defer the commissioning of my younger brother, Giles, until I got back from the colonies. Norbury, the steward, virtually ran both the house and estate, but having Giles there would be a comfort to my mother; he *was* her favourite after all.

'Sir Rupert will always have a special place in my heart, Master Thomas,' Josh said sadly. 'When I turned up in Goostrey all them years ago, an out of work down-and-out with a little child to support, he took me on as a tenant farmer. He didn't know me from Adam but he took me on . . . And later on, although thinking about it now it must have sounded daft at the time, he even went along with my idea of turning the farmhouse into a tavern.'

Josh's words brought me back to earth. Like everyone else who knew him, Josh saw my father as a great humanitarian and an excellent judge of character, which he was, and it was those qualities that had made him a respected landowner and an effective justice of the peace.

'My father was right to back you,' I said. 'Your tavern is a great success because you provide everything a weary traveller needs, a warm, friendly atmosphere and *very* good ale . . . I wish I had a mug of it right now.'

'The stuff they serve in London's like cat's piss, so it is,' Nolan grumbled from the back. 'Still, it's safer to drink than the water.'

'I'm told that chapmen and drovers go miles out of their way to sample your ale, Napper,' I said. 'Tell me, where did you learn the secret?'

For the first time since we set off, Josh's ruddy face creased into a smile. 'Handed down, Master Thomas,' he said. 'The men in the Napper family has always brewed ale. We use oats for the mash and flowers of hopbine from the hedgerows for flavour.' He chuckled. 'Can't tell you no more 'cos it's a family secret, handed down.'

Handed down. The thought hadn't occurred to me, until now. My father was dead; therefore his titles and his estate were now mine, handed down by right of inheritance. I was now a man of property, a landowner — and by God! I was *Sir* Thomas Neville; now that that would take a bit of getting used to.

Our carriage was built for speed. It was

light and well sprung, and on stretches of road that had a good surface we simply flew along. These conditions were rare but it was the weather and not the surface of the road that was slowing us down when we had our one and only brush with a highwayman.

Having dined well and spent a most comfortable night at *The George* in Derby, we awoke to find the weather had deteriorated and it was raining quite heavily. Fortunately the evening before, when leaving the carriage in the yard after stabling the horses, Josh had had the foresight to erect the hood.

We lingered over breakfast but there was to be no let up in the weather so, wrapped in our caped coats and with the brims of our hats pulled down over our eyes, Josh and I took our places on the seat.

Nolan chuckled as he scrambled onto the luggage behind us. 'Sure and this may not be the most comfortable of spots,' he said as he settled himself in, 'but with you two gentlemen sheltering me from the front and the hood up over my head, I'll be as dry as a bone, so I will.'

And so it was that both Josh and I had our heads down against the weather when we heard the cry, 'Stand and deliver!'

'What the devil!' Josh said, reining in the horses.

I looked up into the driving rain. A lone figure on horseback was positioned directly in front of us, completely blocking our path. He too wore a caped coat and a tricorne hat pulled well down. A neckerchief covered the lower half of his face and in his right hand he held a large cavalry pistol, which he was pointing straight at Josh, and at that range he could hardly miss.

'What's up, Major?' a voice behind me said.

'Keep down!' I hissed. 'Do you have your pistols?'

'I do indeed.'

'Load and prime them, quickly. And keep out of sight.'

The highwayman kicked his horse's flanks and moved nearer, still aiming his pistol at Josh. 'Your money, gentlemen, if you please.'

He sounded a well-educated man, a disgraced army officer perhaps or someone from a good family who'd lost heavily at the tables.

'We are just back from the colonies,' I said amiably. 'I would like to help you, old chap, but buying this carriage took all the money we had.'

'Then I'll have your valuables. Empty your pockets.'

I undid my topcoat and made a big show of

trying to extricate my watch from my waistcoat pocket. Exasperated by being kept waiting, the highwayman did just what I was hoping he'd do; he let go of his horse's reins and leaned forward across Josh to grab the fob. Needing no bidding, Josh reached out and grasped the hand holding the pistol. The highwayman, realising his mistake tried to wrest it from him. They struggled and the pistol discharged with a loud report that made the horses whinny and rear up in their traces. Mercifully, the shot went harmlessly over their heads.

'Now *you* stand, me bucko!'

Nolan was on his feet behind me, his feet planted firmly on the luggage, a pistol in each hand pointing at the highwayman.

The would-be robber, having lost his hat and his facemask during his tussle with Josh, now looked a sorry sight. He recoiled violently at the sudden appearance of the ferocious Irishman and then sat back, slumped in his saddle, his shoulders bowed in defeat, his hair clinging to his face in long wet tendrils and the rain dripping from the end of his nose.

'Come on, Napper,' I said. 'Lets get out of here.'

Nolan resumed his seat and the carriage rolled forward. Looking back I saw that the highwayman had dismounted and was scrabbling about in a puddle in the road.

'He's looking for his pistol in the mud,' Josh said with a grin. 'I felt a wheel go over it when we drove off.'

Apart from some urchins throwing stones at the horses as we drove through the pottery towns of Staffordshire the rest of the journey was unremarkable, except perhaps for Holmes Chapel. This small village of less than three hundred souls, still referred to as Church Hulme by some of the older inhabitants, was the scene of much rebuilding activity, the aftermath of a great fire that I later learned had swept through the village a year ago leaving only two cottages, St Luke's church and the Red Lion Inn, standing. The Hall family of The Hermitage, who owned most of the land and other local landowners, including my father, had clubbed together to pay for the rebuilding.

It was getting dark by the time we turned off the London road towards the tiny hamlet of Goostrey. Because of the bad weather and the poor state of the roads in general, our journey from London had taken us almost a week. Emily's ship had sailed nearly two weeks ahead of us and although it had put into New York before crossing the ocean it was only to drop off some barrels of molasses, a task that would have taken no time at all. It had then sailed directly to Liverpool, which was but a day's ride away. So, God willing, Emily should be there ahead of us. In fact, she could have arrived anything up to a month ago.

Josh pulled into his farm and was down from his driving seat and into the tavern almost before the wheels of the chaise had stopped turning. I was in the process of climbing down when I heard a familiar voice behind me.

'Welcome home, Master Thomas. Oh, forgive me, it's *Sir* Thomas now isn't it.' He looked at my face for confirmation that I had received the news of my father's death, and I nodded my head slightly.

I jumped to the ground and turned around. The man behind me moved forward and threw his arms round me in a rib-crushing bear hug. There was a familiar smell of stale tobacco smoke and stable manure about him.

'Sergeant Finch!' I gasped when I got my breath back.

I had missed the old soldier. Had he not promised to take care of Josh's farm and tavern until the innkeeper returned, I would have taken him to the Carolinas without a second thought, and he would have come with me too.

But looking at him now, staring into his tobacco pouch, his iron-grey head bowed, busily filling his pipe to give himself time to get his emotions under control, I saw him as the old man he was. Oh, but he was still fit — and strong! I bet he could still lead two high-spirited horses, one with each hand, although he must be nigh on seventy.

I remember him coming to Dunmere when I was a boy. He had left the army under a cloud. My father said it was over striking a fellow senior NCO for beating a horse. I never did get to know all the details but my father had no hesitation in offering him a position, which proved to me that he believed Finch's side of the story even if his commanding officer didn't.

Nolan, who had sensed this was something of an emotional reunion, went off to find help with the unhitching of the horses.

He reappeared with Elias Leech, who was perhaps the last person I expected to see, and certainly the last person I expected to see working for Sergeant Finch.

The last time I'd encountered the village ne'er-do-well was at Cruikshank's funeral, helping Jed Colclough carry the coffin. He hadn't changed, his eyes were just as shifty and he still had that ever-present irritating smirk on his face. It was as if he knew some dark secret about you. Leech was about ten years older than me, at least two stone heavier, and as far as I knew, hadn't held any job for longer than a week.

A dog followed him from the stables, and next thing there was an excited snuffling around my ankles and little yelps of pleasure as Hagar welcomed me home.

'She's pleased to see you, sir,' said Finch, stating the obvious.

I crouched down to tickle the dog behind its ears and got a licked face for my trouble.

'She looks well, Finch,' I said, straightening up as Leech was leading the first horse away. 'Where's Simon?' I asked, referring to the cantankerous old man Josh had employed for years as his ostler.

'Oh, he's not here, sir. He's retired now and living in one o' they new almshouses of your father's, but he comes in now and then to keep an eye on the ale. He used to help with the brewing, so with Josh away he's taken over, and a good job he's made of it. I don't know what I would have done without him.'

It had been my father's dream that the elderly of the parish should have a place to live; it was another of his 'good works'. Although I had paid to turn his plans into reality I thought it only right that the almshouses should be referred to as being his. I made a mental note to name them Rupert Court, or something like that.

'What's Leech doing here?' I asked.

Finch gave me a wry smile. 'Beggars can't be choosers, sir, labour not being that easy to come by these days. Elias is the only able-bodied man in the village who's not in regular employment. As you know, sir, old Leech was Seth Seaton's cowman, and when he died the cottage was needed for the new man and his family, so Seth had Elias's mother moved into the almshouses. That left Elias without a roof over his head, so he helps me out in the stables in exchange for his food and a bed in the tack room.'

I could just imagine the shiftless Leech still living with his parents. A marriage with a home of his own would mean responsibility, and responsibility was anathema to Elias Leech.

Finch peered at the bowl of his pipe and pushed its smouldering contents down with his thumb. 'He does as he's told,' he said. 'And sometimes it's useful to have a big lad to back you up, like last week when I had to eject the Cleggs.'

'What all of them?' I said jokingly, knowing that Abraham Clegg and his five sons were all big strong fellows. They were knackermen by trade, but rumour had it that by night they were also livestock thieves.

His answer surprised me. 'Aye,' he said, 'all the men of the family that is. Like they was celebrating something. But I think old Simon's ale is a bit stronger than they're used to because the youngest lad, Ethan, he'd only be about sixteen but he's as big as his father, well, he'd had a drop too much and he made a grab at Leila.'

At this I started — so Emily and Leila were here! Finch continued, 'She screamed, a chapman went to her rescue and Abraham floored him. It all happened in a blink of an eye. The peddler only told the lad to let her go but Abraham hit him hard and he went down like a poleaxed bull he did. Then other folk joined in and afore I could get over to stop it there was a right old ruckus going on.

'But don't you worry about Elias Leech. I'll keep my eye on him . . . Everyone deserves a second chance, don't they, Master, er, Sir . . . Oh, damn it! Your father was a great believer in that, take me and Josh for instance.'

We had never talked about his discharge from the army. Although I was curious to hear his side of it, now wasn't the time, so instead I said. 'My father was an excellent judge of character.'

He shook his head sadly. 'Aye. We'll not see his like again. It were a shame you weren't here for the funeral. It were a grand affair, a big turnout. The villagers filled the church-yard and the estate workers lined the route from the Hall to St Luke's church. Colonel Neville brought the twenty-second's band and they played slow-marches all the way. There was a union flag over Sir Rupert's coffin and after the vicar had said his piece a trumpeter sounded a call. Beautiful it was, very moving.'

I should have been there, son and heir and all that. I told myself I'd go to the family vault later and pay my last respects privately, but now I was just as anxious as Josh to get inside that tavern and see Emily!

'Come on Finch,' I said, giving the old cavalryman a playful punch on the arm. 'Let's go and sample Simon's ale. Oh, and by the way, it would seem most odd if you didn't call me 'Master Thomas'. So do that will you? When there's just the two of us, of course.'

I could hear the singing before I reached the door. The taproom of Josh's tavern at this time of the day was never a quiet place but, in my experience, the noise was usually that of many men talking loudly, each intent on having his say and being heard over the conversations going on around him. There was occasional laughter, but never singing.

The sight that greeted me when I opened the door reminded me of that fateful night when I first set my eyes on Edwin Cruikshank. But this was no dandy holding court before an audience of gullible bumpkins but a tall, handsome woman leading a room full of men in song:

'A farmer was ploughing his field one day.'

'*Riteful, riteful, tiddy fie day.*'

'When the devil came up and to him did say.'

'*With a riteful, riteful, tiddy fie day.*

I squeezed my way in. The place was so crowded I couldn't see across the room but I knew that on the far side the barrels would be ranged along the wall, draped with damp cloths to keep their contents cool. And that's where I would find Emily, if she were in the tavern, at the long table filling tankards with ale from a big jug.

'She's good for business that one.' Finch had followed me inside and now stood just inside the door gazing with admiration at the woman who was holding centre stage in that noisy, smoke filled room.

'Leila her name is, Leila Sculley. Came here with Josh's Emily and, as bold as brass, told me I needed a singer in the evenings. Well, as you know, sir, Josh never held with paying entertainers but as she was Miss Emily's friend I said we'd give it a go. As you can see, she's very popular. She sings here every night and with the amount of ale we're selling I can well afford to pay her. Not that she's short of a shilling or two; she's bought that nice little cottage on the Swettenham road, you know, sir, old Widow Harris's place.'

Miss Sculley had the whole room in the palm of her hand. She had positioned herself in front of the huge fireplace, and there, with her skirts lifted tantalizingly above her ankles she was performing a series of dainty steps:

'See here my good man, I have come for your wife.'

'*Riteful, riteful, tiddy fie day.*'

'For she's the bane and torment of your life.'

'*With a riteful, riteful, tiddy fie day.*'

George Whitfield had described her as a 'big woman', and that she was. But she was beautiful, like a Rubens painting. Our eyes met and she smiled. Her smile unnerved me. It was as if she knew everything there was to know about me. And those eyes, where had I seen eyes like that before?

'Come on, sir, follow me,' Finch said, pushing his way through the crowd. 'I'll take you to Emily.'

11

We fought our way to the far side of the room, and in the small space between the barrels and the long table we found Josh and his daughter clasped in each other's arms and weeping tears of joy. Emily's face was buried in her father's shoulder and he was gently stroking her hair and murmuring, 'There, there,' over and over again.

I longed to take her in *my* arms and tell her how much *I'd* missed her but after her terrible experiences at the hands of Cruikshank and Harwood I feared rejection so I put off the moment, telling myself it would be tactless to interrupt such a touching reunion.

I motioned Finch away. 'Let's leave them to it,' I said, 'I can say hello to her later . . . I'll stay overnight if you've got a couple of rooms?'

'I've only got one room occupied — by a tinker, a young fellow called Massey.'

'I thought hawkers and tinkers always slept in the barn?'

'Massey came recommended by Norbury, sir,' he said almost reverently. 'He's done work at the Hall.'

Norbury was something of an institution at Dunmere Hall. He'd been butler there since well before I was born. Now he was the steward, a position he had virtually created for himself. Not that I objected, because with him running the house and estate, and my younger brother looking after my parents, I had been able to leave home with a clear conscience to search for Emily.

Finch was still talking. 'There are some drovers who want to stay tonight but they smells too much like their animals so they'll be sleeping in the barn.' He waved an arm in the direction of the stairs. 'You can go on up if you like, sir. Take the big room at the back. You know the one; you've stayed in it often enough. I'll go through to the kitchen and bring Nolan in that way. It'll be easier for him with the luggage.'

'He will need a room too.'

'Of course, sir. He can take his pick. He'll soon see which room Massey's in, all his stuff's there. The lad will be with us for a while I'm thinking. We nearly had a nasty accident in the kitchen the other day when a handle came off a pan full of boiling soup so I've given him the job of checking everything. I want to make sure that it doesn't happen again.'

'You should get Napper to do it.'

Finch shot me a questioning look. 'Beg your pardon, sir?'

'I'll tell you about it later,' I said, grinning as I made for the stairs.

When I got to the large chamber at the back of the house, I hesitated. The last time I opened this door it was to discover Emily in bed with Cruikshank. The evil priest had been dead now for well over two years and still he could get under my skin. Damn him to hell! I said under my breath, and then I smiled as the thought struck me that hell was the best the Devil could offer his followers in the afterlife.

I flicked up the latch and went inside. A fire was smouldering in the grate. I went over and stirred the logs with the poker until tongues of flame were flickering up the chimney. I positioned a chair in front of the fire and I was in the process of hanging my damp coat over it to dry when there was a tap at the door. Thinking it was Nolan, I carried on draping the coat, at the same time calling out, 'Come in.'

'Mr Finch said there was a gentleman staying in this room and I was to bring him a jug of hot water straight away.'

Emily's voice! My God, it was Emily! I turned round. At the same instant, having placed the jug on the washstand, she turned

131

round also, and suddenly we were face to face.

For what seemed like an age neither of us spoke, and then she said, 'Thomas, by all that's wonderful, it's you, it's really you.' I couldn't help myself and I stepped forward and gathered her in my arms. At that moment I wouldn't have swapped places with King George himself.

I'd journeyed halfway round the world to be with her and now I was actually holding her. I bent to kiss her.

'No, Thomas,' she whispered, wriggling free. 'Not now.'

Seeing my look of bewilderment, she took my hand and led me over to the bed where she sat down and patted the covers beside her for me to do the same. And there she sat, gazing at me, big-eyed, like a frightened doe.

Put me with any group of men, be they nobility or coarse soldiery and I can hold my own but faced with a handsome woman I become a tongue-tied fool.

'I didn't expect to find you here,' she said at length. 'Papa told me you had travelled back together, but I assumed you'd carried on to Dunmere Hall.' Her face clouded. 'Oh, Thomas. I'm so sorry about your father.'

The last thing I wanted was for this precious moment to turn into a wake. I nodded my head sadly, and to change the subject I said the first thing that came in my head. 'I see Milly's still working here.'

Milly was one of Big Ernie Goodrich's daughters. Big Ernie had grown up on the estate and was now one of its tenant farmers. He was a giant of a man and both his daughters took after him in stature. When Finch hired Milly to help him in the tavern after Josh had left it was suggested that it wasn't her skill in pouring ale that got her the job but her ability to handle drunks.

Emily smiled. 'Yes, it was lovely to find her here. She's brought me up-to-date with all the village news.'

Then there was another awkward silence until I said, 'That friend of yours, Leila. She's er, got plenty of energy, hasn't she?'

'Oh, Leila's wonderful, she'd make any party go with a swing.' The smile left her face as she added, 'She's been my rock, Thomas. I think I would have gone mad without her. She saw me through a terrible time and got me back to England. Though where she got the money from for the passage, God alone knows.'

God, and one or two others, I thought, but aloud I said, 'Your father says she's a very determined woman.'

'Oh, yes, once she's made up her mind to

do something there's no stopping her. She said she'd get me back home, and she did. It was as if it were as important to her to get to Goostrey as it was to me.'

There was a sharp knock on the door. 'Begging your pardon, Sir Thomas, but is Emily there?' It was Sergeant Finch.

'Yes, she's here, Finch. Come in.'

The old soldier opened the door cautiously and peered inside. He relaxed visibly when he saw us merely sitting on the bed. Touching his forehead with an extended forefinger, he said, 'Excuse me, Sir Thomas,' (Would I ever get used to the title?) 'I've come to ask Emily to make up the master bedroom for her father. Josh desperately needs to get to bed, sir, he looks worn out.'

Emily was on her feet in an instant. It was as if she was pleased to have an excuse to leave. I was feeling rather tired anyway. 'Go and see to your father,' I said. 'We'll talk again at breakfast.'

Emily left, and Finch was about to follow when he hesitated. 'I've been using Josh's room while he's been away, sir,' he said, by way of explanation. 'I've moved my stuff into one of the guest rooms for now. I'm sorry to drag young Emily away but Milly and me's run off our feet down there. All that singing gives the customers a thirst. It's good for

134

business but it don't half keep you on the go.' He smiled as a thought struck him. 'I'll be able to return to my quarters at the Hall now Josh's back won't I, sir — if that's all right with you?'

'Perfectly, Finch. So long as you remember to bring Hagar with you.'

He went away chuckling to himself.

Relaxed by the warmth of the fire, tiredness began to creep up on me. Nolan arrived with my luggage and I had to mentally shake myself out of my lethargy to ask him if he'd sorted out quarters for himself.

'Indeed I have, sir,' he said. 'The room next to this one was taken so I'm in the one opposite that . . . Can I get you anything before you turn in, sir?'

I told him I could do with a drink but I didn't feel like cold ale or wine. He went away saying he would see what he could find. While he was gone I put more logs on the fire and changed into my nightshirt. The water Emily had brought up was no longer hot but it served to rinse the dust of the journey off my face and hands.

I was drying myself with a towel when Nolan returned bearing a tray, upon which was a cup of steaming liquid and a plate with a cover over it. I thanked him and told him he wouldn't be needed any more that night but at first light he was to ride to Dunmere Hall and tell my mother to expect me.

'Take one of our horses, Finch will find you a saddle. You are to say that I was fatigued after my journey and having stopped at the tavern to let Josh Napper off I decided to rest there for the night before proceeding on to the Hall.'

Nolan's face remained impassive while I was speaking but I thought I saw him smile as he turned to leave.

The hot drink proved to be mulled wine and under the cover was a slice of game pie. Each in its own way full of flavour and deserving to be savoured but I despatched them both quickly as I couldn't wait to get into bed.

I longed to stretch out on a clean, thick, down-filled mattress. Those found in Coaching Inns were usually filled with horsehair (and other things it didn't do to dwell on) but even they were preferable to the hard, wooden bunk I had endured on the *Caprice*. I knew from experience that this bed was the very epitome of softness, and I wouldn't be sharing it with any uninvited guests! I eased myself in, pulled up the covers and blew out the candle.

I had just drifted off to sleep when, in my dreams, a suit of armour toppled over and landed with an almighty crash on a flagstone floor. The noise woke me. Now, someone was clomping about in heavy boots. The noise was coming from the next room and I realised that it hadn't been a dream. It was Massey! I was out of bed like a shot. Recommended by Norbury or not, that tinker needed reminding that he wasn't the only occupant of the guest wing, but when I opened my door I saw that the situation was well in hand. My warm, comfortable bed was calling so I left Nolan to it.

12

The following morning I woke refreshed from a good night's sleep and I was out of bed and partly dressed before my man arrived with my dish of tea and hot shaving water.

Using a corner of the towel, I wiped away the dampness that had formed overnight on the cold windowpane and I was pleased to see that the weather had improved somewhat. At least it wasn't raining.

Nolan had stropped my razor and laid out clean linen so it took but a few minutes for me to complete my toilet and finish dressing.

Big Milly Goodrich was in the taproom when I came downstairs. She had obviously just swept the floor and was now busily scattering fresh sawdust over it. Bidding her a cheery 'Good morning', I made my way to the kitchen. That the innkeeper and the butcher paid Jed Colclough, the village carpenter, good money for the sweepings from his floor only to throw it down on theirs I found quite amusing.

Emily was baking rolls for breakfast. 'I hope you've got some marmalade to go with those,' I said with a smile.

You can keep your cold leftovers from yesterdays meat; give me the bittersweet bite of good orange marmalade on hot, buttered, toasted bread for breakfast. That and tea; I did not subscribe to this newfangled idea of coffee in the morning.

'If you'll take a seat in the taproom. I'll bring it through when it's ready,' she replied without looking up.

I hesitated. 'I was rather hoping you would join me,' I said.

Emily continued to bustle about in the kitchen, rattling in drawers for utensils and banging pots on the stove. 'I had my breakfast with the others,' she said. 'Your man, Nolan, sat with us.'

Having been brought up to not give a thought to those who prepared breakfast it didn't occur to me that Emily would have hers with the rest of the staff. And I never thought I'd be jealous of Barney Nolan.

So, I ate a lonely breakfast. Even marmalade on hot buttered toast failed to lift my spirits.

'Damn it!' I said, striking the table with my fist, bouncing the pots and dishes and causing a knife to fall to the floor with a clatter. I'd fought bloody battles to be with Emily and I'd be damned if I was going to give up trying! I gathered up my dirty crockery, stomped into the kitchen and asked if I could meet her later.

'I've got a busy day ahead,' she said, taking my pots from me and carrying them over to the sink on the far side of the room. 'Leila wants me to take her to the priory.'

The priory! The very name sent shivers down my spine. Once it had been nothing more than a picturesque ruin, rather like the romantic follies everyone seems to be building nowadays, but to me it will always be an ominous reminder of the evil doings of Edwin Cruikshank and his sinister Bucks' Club, the group of rich young wastrels to whom dressing up as monks added spice to their debauchery.

'Why on earth does Leila want to visit the priory?' I asked.

Emily began washing the plates and dishes. She had her back to me so I couldn't see her face. 'She was with me when I gave birth,' she said. 'She asked me who the child's father was and I told her. It was a time for telling the truth.'

'What on earth did you tell her?'

She turned to face me. 'I told her he was a priest — and one of the most handsome men I had ever seen,' she said, a defiant tilt to her chin.

'You said it was a time for telling the truth.

Did you also tell her how he served you when he found you were expecting his child?'

'Oh, yes. I told her how he got rid of an awkward problem by having me put aboard a slave ship bound for the colonies. And I felt a lot better for having told her.'

'So she's your confidante is she, this Leila?' I heard myself say sarcastically. My God! Was I jealous of Leila as well?

She stood with her eyes closed as if making a supreme effort to conquer her emotions. A long moment passed before she said, 'The child died in her arms.'

I felt awful. What the blazes was the matter with me? I wasn't able to say what I wanted to say and what I did manage to say made matters worse. 'You don't have to talk about it,' I said awkwardly.

She rounded on me, her eyes blazing. 'Oh, but I do have to talk about it! Leila Sculley is a remarkable person. She saw me through the worst period of my life and the experience has changed us both, her remarkably so.'

Emily sat at the table. She seemed to be in control of herself now and, I hoped, sorry for her outburst. Clearly there was more she wanted to say, so I said nothing and waited. After a few minutes she looked up at me and said, 'When I first met Leila she slunk around the place like a whipped dog, with her eyes downcast and not speaking to anyone. I soon learned that she too had suffered at the hands of Colonel Harwood and this was why she was so withdrawn. But as she cradled my dying child in her arms an extraordinary change came over her. The heart-rending sadness of the occasion must have unleashed something within her for at the very moment of his death she let out an almighty shout. I couldn't tell you what it was she called out but it was as if she were damning God himself. This sudden release of pent up anger brought her self-confidence back and the change in her personality was truly amazing.

'Since then, Cruikshank has become an obsession with her. It's as if she can't know enough about him. She's always asking questions about him. I told her he'd bought the old priory from your father and used it for the monthly meetings of the Buck's Club, so now we're here she can't wait to see it. There, now you know why Leila wants me to take her to the priory.'

Monthly meetings? Monthly weekends of carousing and debauchery more like, I thought, remembering the sons of some of the richest families from the surrounding counties gathering at the priory, happy to dress as monks and take part in Cruikshank's quasi-religious ceremonies if it meant guzzling his wine and making

142

free with the harlots he provided.

Emily got up and went back to the sink. 'Sergeant Finch said he's buried there,' she said, making such a noise with the pots and dishes that I doubted if any would emerge unscathed from the washing up water. 'Is that right, Thomas?'

'Yes, in the crypt,' I replied tersely. Her questions were provoking memories I didn't want to think about.

It had been a problem to know what to do with Cruikshank's body. He was, after all, an ordained priest and as such my father felt that in spite of his sins he should be buried in consecrated ground but the Reverend Hulse flatly refused to have a practicing Satanist in the churchyard at St Luke's.

I had racked my brain for a possible alternative, eventually coming up with the long-abandoned crypt at the priory. This John Hulse eagerly pounced on, telling my father that to the best of his knowledge it was still sanctified. He was so relieved to be off the hook he even offered to officiate.

So the decision was made. Jed Colclough was instructed to knock up a coffin and Cruikshank was laid to rest with minimal ceremony amid the mouldering bones of long dead monks, the first interment at the priory for over a hundred years.

'You'll not get into the crypt without a key,' I said, 'and that's up at the Hall.' The clattering of dishes stopped and Emily turned around. She looked so disappointed that I found myself saying, 'I'll take you there.'

Her face lit up. 'Today?'

'Tomorrow,' I said. 'I must first pay my respects to my mother.'

★   ★   ★

Finch readily agreed to loan me another saddle, so while the stable lad was getting my horse ready I walked across the tavern yard intent on visiting the family vault at St Luke's.

After the recent rain, the air was fresh and sweet and I stopped just outside the gate to fill my lungs. Somewhere up in the treetops a woodpigeon was hooting in reply to another of his kind in the next field and hidden deep in the tall hawthorn hedges that lined the road, smaller birds marked my presence with hushed twittering. There were other sounds too, recognisable human sounds. The squeaking of the long iron handle as a pail was being filled at the parish pump, and in the distance, the rasping noise of wood being sawn in Jed Colclough's workshop.

'Hello, soldier-boy.'

The voice came from behind me, low and husky, and decidedly feminine. I spun round and our eyes met.

'Megan Griffith!' I gasped.

Only Megan Griffith, or Welsh Meg as she was more commonly known, had the gall to call me, 'soldier-boy'. Regarded as the wicked lady of Goostrey, Megan was tall and slim with wild, flyaway, jet-black hair, a heart-shaped face, high cheekbones and large, spellbinding, brown eyes. A strikingly handsome woman, but to me her most fascinatingly attractive feature was her mouth. It was small with unusually deep laughter lines bracketing its corners and a top lip that projected ever so slightly over the bottom one. The whole effect was that she was both pouting and laughing at you at the same time.

'In the flesh, soldier-boy,' she cooed, striking a Britannia-like pose with the long handled spade and basket she was carrying. 'I knew you were back.'

Megan sold charms and potions, and some folk said she was a witch, a concept she was happy to encourage because, she said, it guarded her privacy. She was also rumoured to sell her favours, but I had no personal knowledge of that.

Any thought of her having had some supernatural premonition of my arrival in

Goostrey was dashed when she continued with, 'You know what this village is like. Nothing much happens here so the word spread like wildfire when your coach was seen turning off the London road.' She handed me the spade. 'Here, help me dig up some horseradish, will you? There should be some here; an inn or a tavern is usually a good place to find it. They makes it into a cordial to revive weary travellers.'

'But won't Napper be angry if we dig up his horseradish?'

Megan laughed. 'The roots travel far under the ground. Josh's will be on his side of the hedge. This side is the King's highway and I can't see His Majesty objecting to us helping ourselves to some of his horseradishes, can you? I'll point them out and you dig them up.'

This mysterious woman intrigued me. 'Your potions are considered to be most efficacious,' I said.

She laughed. 'My mother taught me the medicinal properties of plants and herbs, but most times it's the faith folk have in what I give them that does the job. Take young Jacob Colclough for example.'

'Jed Colclough's son?'

'That's him.' She directed me to a clump of large coarse-looking leaves. 'He learned to swim with the aid of a cork from a bottle of Madeira wine.'

'You've got to be joking!'

'No, seriously. Young Jacob would go along to the millpond with his friends, but while they swam around in the water having a good time he would flounder and go under. So, in desperation he came to see me. I don't know if he expected some sort of magic spell but what he got was the cork on a piece of string to hang around his neck. I told him very solemnly that while he wore it he would never sink.'

'And it worked?'

'Oh, yes. That was last spring. He lost the cork eventually but by then he was a strong swimmer. You see he had the ability but needed to have faith in himself, and that silly cork gave it to him . . . I suppose you've met that Leila person,' she said, changing the subject completely. 'She'll find out one day that there's not room for two of us in a little place like Goostrey.'

I had no idea what she was talking about and I didn't want to know. I worked the spade vigorously into the soil around the root and said the first thing that came into my head. 'Old Brownlow, the gardener at the Hall, told me once that the best time to dig horseradish was after the first frost.'

'That's only if you're going to eat it,' she said with a wink. 'I need this to make a poultice for Seth Seaton's back.'

As I straightened up with the plant in my hand, Megan moved closer and whispered, 'Did you know, soldier-boy, that it's also a powerful aphrodisiac?'

I decided not to walk to St Luke's on this occasion. I said something about my horse growing impatient, thrust the horseradish at her, and beat a hasty retreat.

13

Although I'd only used it as an excuse, I wasn't wrong about the horse. When I got back in the tavern yard I found it saddled up and demonstrating its impatience by scraping its fore-hoof on the ground.

Finch was talking to the boy who was holding the horse's head. They both looked round when they heard my footsteps, and then, out from behind the old cavalryman came Hagar, bounding towards me across the yard.

'The dog is happy to see you, Sir Thomas,' Finch said with a grin. 'I'm still in the process of handing things over to Josh so I'll not be able to get away just yet. Why don't you take her with you?'

'Right, let's go,' I said, swinging myself up into the saddle, and with the dog trotting happily at my side I walked the horse out of the yard and onto the road.

Shielded from the yard by the hedge, Megan blew me a kiss.

Arriving at St Luke's, I left Hagar guarding the horse and went inside to say goodbye to my father. The new plaque on the wall was immediately obvious. Under the de Neville coat of arms was my father's name and title, and under that the simple words, *loved and respected by all*, as indeed he was.

I descended into the gloomy depths of the crypt where time seemed to have stood still for centuries. As I stood before my father's coffin my thoughts drifted to my elder brother's funeral, after which my father had distanced himself from me. I thought at first that he blamed me for Ned's death, as my brother had died as the result of an injury he sustained while we were playing together, but as I grew older I realised that this was his way of coping with his grief. Because of this I had never really got to know my father — and now I never would.

After leaving the church, my journey took me to the crossroads at the edge of the heath where I was relieved to see that the gibbet was empty. Before I left for the Americas, the last occupant of this grisly deterrent to would-be highwaymen and other wrongdoers had been the loose-tongued poacher, Ben Sorrel. Not lawfully executed because of his trade but murdered by the Bucks' Club for telling all and sundry about the strange goings-on he'd witnessed at the priory.

Once out on the windswept heath where nothing taller than gorse will grow, Hagar ran off, searching excitedly for rabbits. I urged my horse into a canter, making for the belt of trees at the edge of the moorland where, over to the left, the top of the crenellated tower of the priory was just visible and on the right, were the tall, twisted chimneys of Dunmere Hall.

There is a wide avenue through the trees and it is from here that the visitor catches their first sight of the large timber framed house that my ancestor, Richard de Neville, built over two hundred years ago as a moated manor with a central courtyard. Over the years, subsequent occupants have stamped their personality on it with various additions and alterations which had resulted in the building one sees today, a rambling, picturesque jumble of pointed gables and overhanging upper stories, its timbers darkened and the plasterwork lime-washed in true 'Cheshire Magpie' tradition.

I was fearful of what would I find when I got there. Under Cruikshank's evil influence, my mother had regressed to being a silly romantic girl. By the time I left she was more like her normal self but still subject to bouts of melancholy. I didn't like to speculate on how my father's death would have affected her.

Crossing the stone bridge that spanned the moat I continued on through the gatehouse

151

arch. It seemed strange not to have Sergeant Finch or a stable lad waiting by the bridge.

The old cavalryman claimed to be able to hear horses approaching a mile off, and for years I believed him until one day one of his lads gave away his secret. It was the dogs that warned Finch and his staff of approaching horses.

Finch was still at the tavern but the reason why there was no one from the stables waiting to help with the horses is because there are no longer any dogs at Dunmere Hall. Dogs didn't like Cruikshank so he'd had them all put down, except Hagar, who Finch had kept hidden in his quarters and was now running between my horse's legs letting out little yelps of pleasure.

Smallwood, the new butler, appeared in the doorway and on seeing who it was arriving, shouted back inside for a footman to come out and hold the horse. The man burst through the portal at a run, and behind him, at a more sedate pace, came the steward, Norbury.

'Welcome home, Sir Thomas,' he said, his normally unemotional face unable to repress a smile. 'We heard you were back.'

Dear old Norbury, I was so pleased to see him I jumped down and went to shake his hand. He backed away. 'Not in front of the staff, sir,' he whispered. 'It wouldn't be seemly.'

Rebuked by the former butler! Well, my mother was always lecturing us boys on the perils of being too familiar with the servants. 'They know their place and they won't thank you for upsetting the order of things,' she would say.

Giles, of course, claimed that the rule didn't apply to the young females on the staff.

Where was he, the young scoundrel? I strode into the great hall calling his name, my voice echoing back from the high arched roof.

Nothing ever changes at Dunmere Hall. The long table, used only on high days and holidays, was still there, as was the screen, behind which were the chamber pots where male guests would relieve themselves during dinner, and my father's chair by the fireplace where he would sit and smoke a pipe before retiring for the night. Even the smell was the same, a mixture of wood smoke and the tangy odour of the rush matting that covered the stone floor. God! It was good to be back home.

'Tom! So here you are then?' Giles came running down the stairs. He looked older somehow, less the young rascal, more the responsible adult. Being in charge these past few months had done him good.

'Young Fletcher, the boot boy, said he saw you driving into Josh's farm yesterday. He's not a full shilling so I didn't know whether to believe him or not until your man arrived this morning.' After a rib-crushing hug, he stepped back with a sly grin on his face. 'Spent the night at Josh's tavern, eh?' he said slyly. 'I bet Emily was pleased to see you.'

I gave him a playful punch on the shoulder. 'She was, as a matter of fact.' I put my arm around his shoulder and led him through to the parlour where I was pleased to see that Smallwood maintained the tradition established in my grandfather's day of leaving some glasses and a couple of bottles of port on a tray for the purpose of welcoming guests and to refresh the weary traveller. Today, the bottles were not from mainland Portugal but from that country's island off the African coast. I could hardly be considered a guest in my own home but I felt I met the requirements of the second category so I poured myself a large glass of the Madeira wine, and one for Giles.

He took it and perched himself on the edge of the table. 'We got worried when Emily came back without you,' he said.

'I wasn't far behind her. I trailed her all the way from Georgia to South Carolina. If her companion hadn't had the money for their passage to England, I'd have caught up with them at Charleston.'

Giles raised his glass. 'Here's to Emily's companion. What a woman! You should see how she packs 'em in at the tavern.'

'I have,' I said. I took a gulp of wine before asking, 'How's mother?'

'Oh, she's quite recovered from her experience with Edwin Cruikshank. In fact she's quite her old self again — so watch out!'

'But Father's death, how did she take that?'

He didn't reply immediately and seemed to be weighing up his answer. 'Reasonably well, considering,' he said at length. 'He went quickly, you see. No lingering deathbed scenes or anything melodramatic like that. Father died in the Orangery, sitting in his favourite seat. His man, Harper, found him. Thought he'd fallen asleep, which he had in a way, I suppose.'

A sad face looked out of place on Giles so, in an attempt to lighten the mood, I changed the subject by asking him about the twenty second.

That did the trick. He grinned broadly. 'I've had an invitation to a dining-in night at the officers' mess this coming weekend,' he said excitedly. 'Now you're home there's nothing to stop me going, is there? I say, perhaps you'd like to come too. I bet Uncle Reuben would be pleased to see you.'

'What's the occasion?' I asked.

'A company of Dragoons are stopping over at Chester barracks for a few days on their way back from Ireland. Should be a jolly night.'

I laughed and shook my head. 'You go by all means, little brother, but I'll give it a miss if you don't mind. Dragoon officers are notoriously heavy drinkers.'

'Thomas! You've decided to come home then.'

My mother swept into the room. Elizabeth Neville was a tall, elegant woman. A gentleman doesn't ask a lady her age but according to my Uncle Reuben, who, as a young man had been in serious competition with my father for her hand, she had been in her teens when she married, so although she must now be well into her fifties she was no dowager. There wasn't a sign of grey in the light brown hair she wore piled high on her head and her lovely cornflower-blue eyes shone as clear and as bright as any young girl's.

She positioned her cheek for me to kiss. As I dutifully did so, she whispered, 'Do send that dog out, Thomas. You know I don't allow animals in my parlour.'

I clicked my fingers and pointed at the open door. Hagar slunk out and lay down in the threshold where she could still see me.

'I saw your man using the main staircase,' she continued. 'Show him where the servant's stairs are and tell him to use them in future, will you, there's a dear?'

Behind her back, Giles gave me a wink. He was right. Mother certainly was her old self and she cut such a regal figure that it was hard to imagine her as the witless waif I'd discovered by the side of the road, picking mushrooms for Edwin Cruikshank's breakfast.

Conscious that we were both holding filled glasses, I asked if I could pour her a drink.

She frowned. 'It's a little early for me, Thomas, but if you care to ring for Smallwood, I will take a small sherry with you. I really do need to talk to you . . . in private,' she added, giving Giles a pointed look.

'Tell you what, Mamma,' he said cheerfully, 'don't let's bother Smallwood, I'll get the sherry.'

Giles left us and I stood sipping my wine waiting to hear what it was my mother had to say to me.

Several long minutes crawled by before she said, 'Thomas, I feel I should tell you this before you learn of it elsewhere.' She turned to look out of the window. 'Edwin Cruikshank advised your father to change his will.'

'And did he?' I asked, wondering where this was leading.

'Oh, yes,' she said matter-of-factly, still gazing into the garden. 'You do not inherit the estate.'

That was so unexpected I had difficulty in believing her. The Nevilles were traditionalists. The title and the estate *always* went together. Giles and I had been brought up to understand that the heir to the baronetcy also inherited the estate in its entirety. My father, as the eldest of two brothers, had done so when he acceded to the title and he made it quite clear to us that our elder brother, Ned, would do likewise. Consequently, it was decided that I would follow my uncle, my father's younger brother, into the county regiment and Giles, a most unsuited candidate for priesthood, had been packed off to a seminary. When Ned died I became the next in line for the title and the estate. At least that is what I had been led to believe.

Damn it all! I'd paid off my father's debts and worked hard to get the estate back on a sound business footing again before I left for the Americas.

'So, who has he named in his will?' I asked, bleakly.

My mother turned to face me. 'Your father remembered everyone, Thomas,' she said, in a tone of voice that took me right back to my nursery days. 'All the servants, from Norbury to the boot boy, are to receive a small legacy, and of course, you and Giles get your pick of his guns and horses . . . '

'But the *estate*, Mother?'

'Goes to me.'

It was a bolt from the blue that left me speechless.

'But I want you to run it as if it were your own, Thomas, as it will be when I go to join your father.'

Before I could marshal my thoughts to reply, Smallwood appeared and she went off with him to deal with some household emergency.

Giles appeared on the threshold holding a glass and decanter. 'Hello, Mamma gone has she?' He stepped over Hagar and advanced into the parlour.

'According to her, I'm not to inherit the estate,' I said, still dazed by the unexpectedness of it all.

'I can't believe that!' He poured the sherry into the glass, sipped it and nodded his head approvingly. 'The estate passes to the next in line along with the title, always has, always will.'

'That's what I thought,' I said. 'In fact I remember when Ned died, Father sitting me down in his study and gravely telling me that I was now his heir, and that one day all the Neville land and the people on it would be my responsibility. A stewardship, he called it, a sacred trust.'

Giles looked up with a grim smile. 'I bet this was Edwin's doing.'

'It was. Mother said as much.'

'The crafty beggar! He took me in as much as anyone, more perhaps, and I get so angry when I think of what he did to Father. He turned a level-headed, no-nonsense magistrate into a wild, gambling drunkard. He got him so the old boy would sign anything after a couple of bottles of Port. See the lawyers, Tom. Contest the will.'

'There's no need for that. Mother doesn't want the estate. She said she'd like me to run it as if it were mine.'

'But it's your inheritance, Tom.'

'It still is. She's leaving everything to me . . . So Father and all the dead Nevilles can rest easy in the knowledge that the title and the estate will be reunited once more.'

'And she's definitely going to do that, is she?'

'She said she is, and if you can't trust your own mother who can you trust?'

14

The following morning Nolan set off back to the tavern with instructions to return the saddles to Finch and to come back with Emily and Leila Sculley in the chaise.

I asked Norbury to let me have the keys to the priory. He brought them to me in the great hall with a warning. 'Do have a care, Sir Thomas. The new owner has yet to take possession but I've heard tell of some activity there of late. The curate of Marton church went to look at the building — I'm told he's something of a student of ecclesiastical architecture — and he swears he heard a man's voice coming from the chapel. A voice raised in what sounded to him like a Gregorian chant.'

'Who the devil was it?'

'Precisely, sir. The young man didn't stay to find out. He'd heard about the Black Mass being held there, and fearing it was something diabolical he left in rather a hurry.'

'Probably the wind moaning through the cloisters,' I said.

My little brother appeared at the doorway. 'Or the curate had been at the sacramental

161

wine!' he said with a grin.

Although now my equal in height, I still think of Giles as my 'little' brother.

'Who owns the priory now?' I asked him when Norbury had left.

'Cruikshank's crony, Sir Vivian Rushford. The rogue priest left him everything apparently.'

'But we still have the keys?'

'Oh, yes. No one's seen Rushford since the day Cruikshank died. He lives down south. Somewhere in the Chilterns, I think. He's probably scared of showing his face around here in case you set that big fellow on him again.'

'Daniel Coggins?'

'That's him. Why this sudden interest in the priory?'

'I'm going there today. With Emily and her friend Leila. It appears the woman is fascinated by Cruikshank, so I'm taking her to see his coffin.'

Giles whistled. 'That'll be a jolly outing. Now if you were planning to sit by the side of the mere with a basket of food and a couple of bottles of wine I'd come with you, but to gawp at a coffin, ugh!'

It suddenly occurred to me that by having Giles there to divert Miss Sculley, I could possibly get Emily on her own for a few moments. 'We may well do that afterwards,' I said. 'And you'd be very welcome to come along, old chap. You can always stay with the carriage while we're in the crypt.'

Taking a fresh pipe from the rack on the mantelshelf, Giles began stuffing the bowl with tobacco from my father's jar that still stood there. 'Nolan told me about the pirates and the French soldiers,' he said. 'You've done it again, haven't you?'

'What do you mean, 'done it again'?'

Reaching down he held a splinter of kindling to the fire until the end burst into flame. 'Well, you go to India, you rescue the daughter of a wealthy merchant and come home a rich man.' He stood up. 'Then off you go to the Carolinas to look for Emily Napper and you save your ship from pirates and send a platoon of French infantry packing!'

'I didn't get the girl,' I said with a rueful smile.

Giles held the flame to the bowl of his pipe and sucked at the long, clay stem until he was rewarded with a mouthful of smoke, which he proceeded to puff up the wide chimney. He threw the sliver of wood into the fire and turned to look at me, an expression of genuine admiration on his cheerful face.

'When we were children, you showed me the best places to fish and how to snare a rabbit. Now I'd really appreciate a few tips on soldiering before I go off to Chester barracks.'

'The best advice I can give you,' I said, 'is to lead by example — and get yourself some good sergeants.'

At that moment Smallwood appeared announcing the arrival of Nolan and the chaise.

'I thought it best to ask the er, ladies, to remain in the carriage, sir,' he added.

I exploded. 'The devil you did! Fetch them in man, and offer them some refreshment.'

'In *here*, sir?'

'Of course.'

'But her ladyship, sir?'

'Those are my instructions, Smallwood.' The butler's face remained impassive. 'Yes, sir,' he said, and left.

Giles wagged the stem of his pipe at me. 'You'll be in trouble if Mamma finds a serving wench and an entertainer from the tavern supping tea in the great hall.'

I'd never thought of Emily as a serving wench. But he was right, of course. My mother would expect them to be shown to the servants' hall. 'They're *my* guests,' I said truculently, 'and this is *my* house.'

My little brother grinned. 'Not according to what you've just been telling me about Father's will.'

As it happened, my mother didn't come into the great hall while our female visitors were there but that didn't stop me being on tenterhooks the whole time.

Having never set foot in Dunmere Hall before, Emily's jaw dropped when she was shown into the great hall. I offered her a chair and she sat as if in a trance. Had I not hurried her, she would have been content to sit and gaze for hours, as would Giles, although the object of his gazing was not the surroundings but Leila Sculley.

And gaze he might for Emily's friend looked stunning in an open-fronted, full-skirted dress in striped cotton, which she wore with a low cut stomacher and a small hat with a large feather. It was an ensemble that could have only come from one of the most exclusive fashion houses in Charleston.

I limited everyone to one small dish of tea and then bundled them back out to the chaise, where Nolan was waiting for us. He told me later that he had been treated 'right royally' in the kitchen, having been given a tankard of ale and a slice of rabbit pie.

It was but a short ride to the priory. When we came to a halt in front of the old building's impressive façade, I noticed a number of wheel ruts in the soft ground, considerably more than would have been

165

made by the cleric from Marton on his recent visit.

I got down from the chaise and held out my hand to assist Emily who had been sitting behind me, while Giles, on the other side, took Leila by the waist and lifted her down, seemingly without effort. 'As light as thistledown,' the flatterer said, although I saw him flexing his shoulders afterwards when he thought no one was looking. Then, just as we were about to set off, he said, with the air of a martyr, 'Someone has to stay with the horses. You go off and enjoy yourselves. I'll wait here.'

Leaving the young rascal sitting with his feet up in the back of the chaise, I led the way with Nolan and the ladies a pace behind me. In one hand the Irishman held a length of resinous pinewood, its end wrapped with cloth soaked in beeswax, the other he kept in his coat pocket where, I guessed, he carried a pistol.

'*Fais ce que voudras*,' Leila read, looking up at the inscription carved in the stone lintel over the door. 'Do what you will.'

'You speak French?' I asked.

She shook her head. 'No, I just seem to know what it means,' she said with a puzzled look on her face.

I unlocked the entrance door, and with the

166

others following close behind, I made my way along the passageway to the set of double doors, beyond which was the chapel. I hesitated remembering the night we had burst in on a satanic mass to rescue my mother, the night Cruikshank had died. Breathless with excitement, Leila whispered, 'Go on,' and Emily giggled nervously. I pushed open the doors.

Inside the large chamber it was quite gloomy, the only light being that filtering in through the stained glass windows. The smell of incense hung in the still air. I looked toward the high altar, and there, painted on the floor in front of it, was the pentacle, the five-pointed star within a circle of strange words and symbols, and upon the altar stood the black candles and the inverted crucifix.

This was where Cruikshank had died. Behind me I heard Nolan whisper, 'Holy Mother of God.'

Without a word, Leila left us and walked up the aisle. She then stood before the altar with her head bowed as if in prayer. I didn't like to disturb her but Emily looked uneasy and Nolan was obviously anxious to get on, so leaving them standing in the doorway, I went up to Leila and gently tapped her on the shoulder.

To this day I don't know if what followed

really happened but it seemed that Leila turned to face me, her eyes burned in a face that was without expression. '*Enter the pentacle at the risk of your immortal soul,*' she said. But it wasn't her voice, it was a man's voice; it was Cruikshank's voice.

I quickly looked round to see if the others had heard it, but they had gone. When I turned back Leila had turned away and was again facing the altar. 'Miss Sculley?' I said.

She straightened up. 'Why, Sir Thomas. I didn't know you were there,' she said brightly, and looking beyond me into the empty chapel, added, 'I think we should join the others, don't you? They appear to have left.'

We found Emily and Nolan waiting outside in the corridor. My valet's face lit up when he saw us. 'Thank God you're out of there, sir. That place is evil, so it is.'

Emily tugged at my sleeve. 'Let's go and see this wretched coffin and get it over with. This place makes my flesh creep.'

I couldn't have agreed more. Nolan got busy with his tinderbox and when the torch was burning well we set off for the crypt.

This part of the building had escaped the building's refurbishment but although the long plate was corroded with rust the key turned easily in the lock. I pushed open the door.

168

Immediately, my nostrils were filled with the musty smell of death and decay. Beyond the small area illuminated by Nolan's torch everything was in darkness but knowing exactly where Cruikshank's coffin was located I went straight to it, my footsteps sounding unnaturally loud in the deathly silence.

None of us who attended Cruikshank's funeral had wanted to spend more time than was absolutely necessary in this grim place, and as the ledges around the walls of the crypt appeared to be full of other caskets in various states of decomposition, we had left the wooden box containing the priest's mortal remains resting on a pair of Colclough's trestles, not far from the entrance. The coffin was still there but there was something different about it. I beckoned Nolan to come nearer with the flaming torch.

He stepped forward, instantly voicing what was wrong. 'Holy Mother of God! The lid's gone.'

Cautiously, I peered inside. 'And so has Cruikshank,' I said.

Behind me, Emily let out a sob of fear and I turned just in time to catch her as she swooned. Leila tore the feather from her hat and singed it in the flame of the torch. She then wafted it under her friend's nose until, after a little cough and a shake of the head,

Emily opened her eyes. Then, refusing offers of help from both Nolan and me, the big woman pulled Emily to her feet and with one strong arm around her waist they made for the door together.

Emily walked as if in a dream, her face totally devoid of expression. In complete contrast, her friend was animated; her piercing eyes shining with excitement.

Giles waved to us from the carriage but his smile quickly faded when he saw Leila supporting Emily and Nolan with his pistol in his hand.

'What the devil's happened?' he asked, leaping down to help the ladies into the chaise.

Nolan crossed himself. 'That may be nearer the truth than you think, sir,' he said.

I waited until Emily and Leila were settled before answering Giles's question. Walking him out of earshot, to where Nolan was checking the horses' harness, I said, 'Cruikshank's body has gone.'

He looked at me incredulously. 'Are you sure?'

'Nolan was with me. He'll verify that the coffin was empty.'

'It was that, sir,' the Irishman confirmed. 'The lid was off and the reverend was gone, so he was.'

'There! What do you make of that?' I

asked. Then, before Nolan could move away, I grabbed him and said, 'And I'll thank you not to frighten the ladies with any more of your superstitious nonsense.'

'But you've got to admit, Tom,' Giles said, 'first the curate's story of someone chanting in a supposedly empty chapel and now Cruikshank's body's vanished . . . You must admit it is a bit strange, to say the least.'

Nolan's eyes grew wider. 'Someone was chanting in the chapel? Holy Mother of God! What *is* going on here, sir?'

'Something's going on for sure,' I said, 'and whatever it is, I intend to get to the bottom of it. But don't forget what I said, Nolan, don't go frightening the ladies, particularly Miss Emily.' Turning to my brother, I added, 'Her friend seems singularly unaffected by it all. In fact I'd go so far as to say she was enjoying the situation.'

Giles shrugged his shoulders. 'Well, she doesn't know the people involved, does she?' he replied dismissively.

Emily appeared to be in a state of shock so I instructed Nolan to drive directly to Josh Napper's farm and to make all possible speed. The surface of the heath was firm and relatively flat and, being common land, the grass was kept short by the villagers' live-stock. I felt that any hazards should be visible

171

at an avoidable distance and the leather straps supporting the body of the chaise would absorb any bumps we did encounter. As it turned out, apart from scattering a flock of sheep our journey was without incident.

Josh met us in the yard, and after taking one look at his daughter, ordered her straight to bed, asking Leila to go with her. 'I'll be there in a moment,' he called after her. 'I just need a word with Sir Thomas.'

He waited until the girls had gone before saying, 'Sebastian's a sensible fellow. I can't understand why he would take on a villain like Elias Leech.'

I really couldn't see Sergeant Finch as a 'Sebastian' but Josh obviously had more to say, so I said nothing and let him continue.

'I caught the scoundrel selling a cask of ale to some drovers we had sleeping in the barn,' he said angrily. 'And when I mentioned it to Milly she said he'd done it afore! She said she'd seen a carter from Middlewich leaving here with a couple of our casks on his wagon. When she challenged him he said Leech had sold it to him. Leech confessed and begged her not to tell Sebastian, promising not to do it again. Well he has, so I told him to pack his bags and go. Makes you wonder how many casks have gone the same way, don't it?'

He looked down and fiddled with his

apron. I wondered what was coming next.

'Would you stop by your father's almshouses on your way to the Hall, sir?' he asked, 'and see if Simon will come back for a day or so. With Sebastian gone I need someone in charge of the stables. Tell him it's only 'til I find someone regular.'

I readily agreed and Josh steadied the horses while we climbed back on the box.

'Oh, by the way,' I said, 'I asked Sergeant Finch why he gave Leech a job. He said he was giving him a second chance, but he would need watching. I'm surprised he didn't tell you that before he left.'

Josh fiddled with his apron again. 'Well I can't be everywhere . . . '

Satisfied that I had successfully defended my old tutor, I told Nolan to drive on.

15

'Thomas Neville, you are thirty-four. It's high time you were married!'

Giles was right; Mother *was* her old self again.

Shortly after he and I had returned to Dunmere Hall, Smallwood informed me that Lady Neville required my presence in the withdrawing room.

'I've invited Mistress Bottomley to take tea with me,' she announced, 'and I've asked her to bring her charming daughter with her. Now, what *is* her name?'

She was pretending not to remember, I can always tell. 'Prudence,' I mumbled, shuddering as I recalled the tall, gawky girl with large teeth who'd clung to me like a limpet at the last Hunt Ball.

Mother smiled patronisingly. 'That's right, dear,' she purred. 'They'll be here at half past three.'

'But Mother . . . '

'But nothing, Thomas. Just *think* for a moment. Jeremiah Bottomley owns most of the land between here and the River Tame. He has no male heir and his daughter is rather taken with you, her mother told me so.'

I'd had enough of this. 'As you said yourself, mother, I am thirty-four. A little too old for you to be telling me what to do, don't you think?'

I went to the side-table and poured myself a glass of whisky. Not that I needed a drink nor did I like whisky all that much, but it seemed a manly thing to do.

'Being the heir to an estate brings with it certain responsibilities,' she lectured. 'I'm sure your father must have told you that . . . Don't you see, Thomas, this is a golden opportunity to almost double the size of the Neville estate.'

'I'll not marry someone I don't love,' I said firmly.

She laughed. 'Romantic stuff and non-sense! Do you think the shepherdess will marry the penniless farmhand? Not on your life! She'll marry the old farmer who's got a warm house and plenty of food on his table. Or perhaps the princess will marry the handsome troubadour? Not a chance! Her Royal Highness will be married off to a foreign prince to cement an alliance between their two nations . . . Oh, the princess will take her handsome troubadour with her, and *not* just for her guitar lessons, let me tell you. And the shepherdess will continue to meet the farmhand, somewhere where the only witnesses to their lovemaking are her sheep. Wake up to reality, Thomas. Amuse yourself with this serving wench if you must, or any other young lady that takes your fancy, but society demands that you marry someone of your own class.'

I was about to say that neither Emily nor I would be a party to such an arrangement when Giles burst into the room.

'Ah, there you are, Thomas — oh, hello, Mamma — I say, Thomas, d'you think your man would work his magic on my boots? Yours always have such a magnificent shine.' He moved closer, lowering his voice so our mother wouldn't hear. 'Just between you and me, do you soldiers really use spit?' he asked confidentially.

A cunning plan began to form in my mind. 'Yes, we do, old chap. The secret is to take a dab of blacking on a soft cloth, spit on the leather and work the blacking gently in little circles with your finger. You'll get the hang of it when you go to the regiment. The drill sergeant will probably do the same to you as he did to me, and that's to shine one of your boots for you and then leave you to get the other one up to the same standard.'

'I'll be no good,' Giles said glumly. 'I've tried and tried. I either end up with too much blacking and not enough spit, or the other way round. It just doesn't work for me.'

'It will, don't worry,' I said, with a reassuring smile. 'Anyway, you'll only have to clean your own boots during your training. Once that's over you'll have a servant to do it for you.'

'Like Nolan?'

'Yes, just like Nolan. Listen, I'll get him to clean all your boots — *and* teach you how to do it, on one condition.'

His face lit up. 'Anything, Tom. Just name it.'

'Take afternoon tea with Mother and me,' I announced.

'Done!'

My mother looked up in surprise. 'But, Thomas!' she gasped.

'No buts, Mother, remember? I'll be happy to join you for afternoon tea if Giles comes too.'

She glowered at me. 'Oh, very well,' she said.

The guests arrived at the appointed time and, as it turned out, I found the occasion quite entertaining. Well, to begin with anyway.

My scheming parent scowled at me while she was pouring out the tea but once she got talking with the equally voluble Mistress Bottomley she seemed to completely forget about me, as together they began to eagerly dissect a mutual acquaintance, a certain Lady Arabella Warblington, whose boast apparently was that only the most noble people came to *her* dinner parties. And as for Giles, in no time at all he had the eligible daughter eating out of his hand, literally. There he was, totally oblivious to her braying laughter, feeding her cake liberally coated with his honeyed compliments.

Put my little brother in a room with an unattached female and he changes into another person. His voice drops an octave and he becomes suave and debonair. Prudence absolutely lapped it up, as I knew she would, leaving me free to enjoy cook's homemade scones.

An almost continuous soft, silky murmur from Giles and an occasional giggle from Prudence was all I heard from that side of the room, but their mothers made up for it with their incessant chatter. I wasn't really listening but I couldn't help picking up the occasional word here and there. I pricked up my ears though when I heard my name mentioned.

'I was sure Thomas would want to meet him, having just returned from the Americas himself.' This was Prudence's mother talking. 'When Roly told his father he had business in

Cheshire, he asked him to deliver a letter to Sir Henry Mainwaring at Peover Hall. He's gone there now but he'll stop here later to pay you his respects before accompanying us home. I *knew* you wouldn't mind, Elizabeth.'

'Of course not,' my mother replied. 'You'd be interested in meeting someone from the colonies, wouldn't you, Thomas?'

My mouth was full of scone, so all I could do was smile and nod my head in agreement.

'There, I thought he would,' Prudence's mother said. 'You'll like him, Thomas. His father's an Earl you know.'

'Really!' Mother said with enthusiasm. 'And he's a relation of yours?'

'A cousin, a distant cousin, you understand. The family seat is in Wiltshire but, being the third son, Roly went off to the colonies where, by all accounts, he's done really well. He's got a plantation in the country and a beautiful townhouse. And, would you believe, he's even got his own regiment of militia.'

Suddenly, I had a feeling like someone was pouring cold water down my back. I told myself it couldn't be him, could it? Wouldn't that be too much of a coincidence?

'What's his name, this colonial cousin of yours?' I asked with some trepidation.

'Roly, er, Roland Harwood.'

Damn him! He must have followed Leila to retrieve his gold.

He would easily have found out from the garrulous harbourmaster that two ladies had sailed on the schooner bound for Liverpool, and that same man also knew that their ultimate destination was to be Goostrey village in the county of Cheshire.

But Major Reid said the gold was in a small leather bag. Would a small leather bag hold enough gold to warrant the time and expense of travelling to England, particularly as Leila had obviously dipped into the bag to pay for their passage?

My God! Could revenge rather than retrieval be the reason for him being here?

'Roly is such a charming man,' Mistress Bottomley was saying. 'Of course, I'd never met him before, or any of his family come to that. One rarely goes to Wiltshire, does one? He arrived with a letter of introduction from his father asking if he might stay for a few days whilst he conducts business in the area. Well, one can't say no to a relative, can one?'

Giles took a break from whispering endearments to ask what her cousin's business in Cheshire was. My mother signalled her disapproval of his straightforwardness with a haughty sniff, chiding him with, 'Really, Giles. It's not polite to ask such questions.'

Her friend came to his defence. 'That's quite all right, Elizabeth,' she said. 'It's no secret. Roly is here to find someone he knew in Carolina. That's all.

I was just about to make my excuses and leave but it was too late. Smallwood came in to announce the arrival of Mistress Bottomley's distant cousin.

No one would have guessed that this was Roland Harwood's first time at Dunmere Hall. He strode into the room with the assurance of a regular visitor.

'Lady Neville,' he said, bowing low and sweeping his black, satin-trimmed tricorne in an exaggerated arc in front of his outstretched leg. Turning to face the rest of the assembly, he repeated the performance, reciting, 'Ladies and gentlemen,' as he did so. Then, to me, he said, 'When my dear cousin told me we were to visit Dunmere Hall, the home of the Nevilles, I hoped I would be meeting you again.'

Even out of uniform Harwood was elegant. Today he was wearing a light blue coat, a white waistcoat, white satin breeches and white stockings. His shoes were adorned with large silver buckles that complimented the silver buttons on his coat. On his head he wore a powdered peruke with side curls and a pigtail tied with a velvet bow.

Giles and I stood up. I could see my little brother was impressed. As for me, striking the arrogant rogue in my mother's drawing room was unthinkable but the urge to do so took a great effort on my part to resist.

'I believe you're here looking for a friend from Carolina,' Giles said, after shaking Harwood's hand, a custom I managed to avoid on this occasion.

'Hardly a *friend*,' the colonial replied. 'Someone who used to be in my service. I was told she travelled to Goostrey village with a girl I only know as Emily.'

Damn Mackay! Harwood knew everything. If he went anywhere near Emily I'd kill him. That's if her father didn't kill him first.

'Emily?' Giles said, grinning like a fool. 'Tom knows Emily, don't you Tom?'

Giving my little brother a withering look, I said, 'I'm sure Mr Harwood is not talking about the same person.'

Giles caught my eye and remained silent, albeit with a puzzled look on his face. Harwood smiled. 'It's hardly likely, Mr Neville,' he said. 'For this girl is of mixed race, a runaway slave.'

'*Sir* Thomas,' I growled belligerently.

With a cynical smile, he bowed and said, 'Forgive me, Sir Thomas, I didn't know. One should always endeavour to give a person their correct title, don't you think? Mine is the *Honourable* Roland.'

Mistress Bottomley sat looking at him admiringly, her eyes shining with excitement. 'This runaway slave shouldn't prove too difficult to find,' she said. 'Not in a little village like Goostrey. And will she lead you to your quarry — another female you said?'

'Yes, madam,' he replied. 'An indentured servant by the name of Leila Sculley. She has stolen something of great value and importance from me, but I have every confidence I shall recover it very soon. I have a most meticulous man making enquiries for me at this very moment.'

'And who might that be,' I asked.

Harwood dabbed at his nose with an embroidered kerchief as if he had encountered an unpleasant smell. 'A local fellow by the name of Elias Leech,' he replied. 'He warrants he'll track down my property in no time, and I feel sure he will. I have every confidence in him'

Giles was bursting to say something. He shot a glance at me and, observing my frown, bit his knuckle and kept quiet.

Mistress Bottomley stood to take her leave. When freed from her visitor's embrace, my mother rang for Smallwood who appeared so quickly I got the feeling he must have been stationed outside the door. Prudence and Giles exchanged a long lingering look, Harwood executed another of his sweeping bows, and they were gone. My mother, as always, the perfect hostess, escorted them to the entrance hall.

'What the devil's going on, Tom?' Giles fired at me as soon as we were alone.

I quickly outlined the part Harwood had played in the lives of Emily and Leila back in Carolina, ending with: 'So you see why I don't want him to find them.'

'My God, Tom. I'm surprised you didn't call him out.'

'Had there not been ladies present I wouldn't have afforded the scoundrel the courtesy of a duel.'

Giles picked up the last remaining scone, and holding it in his hand, he gazed at it, savouring the prospect of sinking his teeth into the small, lightly sweetened cake.

'What do you think Elias Leech is playing at?' he said absently. 'He knows exactly where Emily and Leila are. He could have told Harwood straight out.'

'Leech is no fool, Giles. He's probably thanking his lucky stars that it was he that Harwood asked first. Had it been anyone else in the village the *Honourable* Roland would have been directed straight to Napper's tavern with no hesitation — and anyone there could have told him where Leila lives.

'No, I bet Leech rubbed his hands together when Harwood stopped to speak to him. And being a quick thinker, he would know that simply sending Harwood to the tavern would be worth sixpence at best; but as Harwood's agent he could well earn himself a guinea.'

'You said Leila stole a bag of gold,' Giles said.

Having demolished the scone he was now wiping his mouth and fingers with a napkin.

'When Leech finds it, what's to stop him grabbing a handful for himself?'

'Nothing, but I doubt if it contained more than that to start with. No, brother of mine, there's something else in that bag, something that's more valuable than gold to the Honourable Roland Harwood, and I'm going to find out what it is. Are you with me?'

16

There was much activity when Giles and I arrived at the stables.

Coggins and Fowler were there together with the trunk from the ship. As I'd paid for the horse and the wagon that had brought them all the way from London, I gave the combination a quick inspection. I judged the sturdy cart to be a most useful vehicle to have on the estate and there was always work for a strong horse so, like the chaise, there would be no hurry to sell either. In fact, I was quite pleased with Fowler's purchase and I made a note to congratulate the little Cockney as soon as he and Coggins were free from the noisy, three-way backslapping reunion they were engaged in with Sergeant Finch.

'I been starin' at a horse's rear end all the way from London,' I heard Fowler complain to Finch. 'Still, I suppose you're used to that, you 'avin' been in the bleedin' cavalry.'

'*My* rear end is numb from sitting on that hard driving seat,' Coggins grumbled. 'The thought of being stuck on that boat for weeks on end was bad enough, but driving a horse and cart up the length of the country is the most boring thing I've ever done. Why did I ever leave the army?'

Hagar was running round the trio and barking with excitement. It was she who saw me first and came bounding over, alerting them to my presence.

'Here we are, Major, at long last,' Fowler called out. 'We was days on that bleedin' boat, but we did as you said and went ashore a lot, and as we weren't all that far from Limehouse, I took Dan to meet my family. We 'ad a right old time, didn't we mate?'

Finch whispered something in the little man's ear.

'Bloody 'ell!' Fraser gasped. 'I'm sorry, sir, I forgot you was a proper 'sir' now. Calling you 'Sir Thomas' will take a bit of getting used to.'

The look of concern on his ferret-like face made me smile. ''Major' will still be perfectly all right from you two,' I said. 'When you've offloaded the trunk and seen to the horse, get yourselves a meal from the kitchen and tell Smallwood you're to have your old room in the gatehouse. My brother Giles and I are going out, so I'll see you when we get back. In the meantime get some rest, both of you, you look tired out.'

My horse threw a shoe on the journey to Leila's cottage so I had to walk him the last mile or so. Giles dismounted and walked with me. The sun had gone down and it had turned quite cold.

The cottage was tied to one of the farms on the estate and had for years been the home of the Harris family until Ben Harris died last year and his widow had moved into the new almshouses.

On the way, Giles had been telling me how happy Leila said she was living there. She was renting the cottage until it was needed again to house a farm worker. Until then it was her very own place and she loved it, he said.

We left our horses tied to the gate and walked up the gravel path to the front door. I was about to knock when I saw it was ajar. Pushing it fully open we went in, calling out Leila's name.

A large log fire was burning merrily in the hearth but the place looked as though it had been hit by a violent storm. Papers and books were scattered everywhere, furniture was tipped over and rugs had been pulled up from the floor.

'In here, Tom,' Giles called from somewhere down the hall. 'In here, quickly.'

I followed the sound of his voice and found myself in a small kitchen. The sight that greeted me was of cupboard doors wrenched off and drawers pulled out and their contents thrown on the floor. Storage jars and baskets had been emptied and cooking pans were strewn everywhere.

Giles was on the far side of the room. He was kneeling down but I couldn't see what he was examining as my view was blocked by a dresser that had been pulled away from the wall and tipped on its side.

Broken earthenware pots crunched beneath my boots as I squeezed past the obstruction. It was then that I saw what it was Giles kneeling beside. It was Leila.

She was lying curled up in a foetal position with her hands tied in front of her with a length of coarse rope, the end of which was frayed as though it had snapped. Her poor face was ashen and mottled with dark bruises. Her lips were cut and swollen, and one eye was so puffed-up that had she been conscious she couldn't have opened it.

Her bodice was unlaced, no, the lacing had been cut and the lilywhite skin of her back was a mass of bleeding lacerations. My scant medical knowledge told me the dead don't bleed, so at least she was alive — thank God! I'd seen many a back after a flogging, but they had all been tough, muscular backs of sailors. I'd never before seen the soft skin of a woman's back broken and cut to bloody ribbons.

189

Giles pointed up at the ceiling where there were hooks for hanging hams and such. A length of rope similar to that around Leila's wrists was tied to one of them.

'The bastards must have hung her there to flog her,' he said with emotion.

'I'd say these injuries were caused by a switch rather than a lash,' I replied. 'See if there's a kettle on the stove. I need salt, some warm water and a cloth to bathe these cuts.'

I leaned forward to untie her, so that I cold roll her over to treat her wounds. As I was undoing the knots, she groaned. The good eye opened blearily, and seeing someone bending over her she drew away.

'Leila, this is Thomas. Giles is here with me. You're safe now.'

'Giles,' she murmured.

My little brother heard her breathe his name. 'I'm here, Leila,' he said tenderly. 'We need to roll you over so that Thomas can tend to your wounds.'

He took over the removal of the rope from her wrists and then, as gently as we could, we turned her onto her stomach. This produced more groans and some words that I hadn't heard since I'd left the twenty-second.

I then bathed the cuts on her back, keeping her talking to prevent her from passing out as I sponged the lacerated flesh.

190

That Roland Harwood had been involved in this terrible thing didn't surprise me. Apparently he had burst into the cottage with the Cleggs, and it was they who had ransacked the place and carried out the beating.

'Harwood gets other people to do the dirty work,' she said. 'But he likes to watch.'

I gently patted her back dry with a towel and she sat up to allow me to bandage it as best I could with strips torn from a clean tablecloth that I'd found on the floor. As I did so, I couldn't help thinking that it is much easier to bandage a man's back than a woman's.

'Did he find what he was looking for?' I asked.

Leila slipped her arms into her dress and pulled it up over her chest. She tried to smile but this was obviously painful and caused her to wince. 'The only thing Harwood took away with him was the contents of a bottle of Megan Griffith's elderflower wine. The damn fellow stood sipping it while Abraham Clegg was flogging me. Clegg was trying to get me to tell him where I'd hidden the bag of gold while his sons went about destroying my home. Harwood finished the whole bottle before I passed out.'

'So it was Abraham who whipped you,'

Giles said angrily. 'I'll whip *him* when I see him.'

Leila did her best to smile. 'You don't have to worry about Abraham Clegg, darling.' A sudden spasm of pain shot through her body, leaving her panting for breath. She looked up at me, fixing my eyes with a stare that plumbed the very depths of my soul and I seemed to hear Cruikshank's voice saying, '*Abraham Clegg is a dead man walking.*'

She shuddered, and the weird, ungodly light vanished from her eyes as quickly as it had come. Her head slumped forward, her chin resting on her chest. The moment had passed.

'My God, Tom. Is she all right?' Giles whispered anxiously.

I tried to sound casual. 'She's swooned, that's all. Only to be expected, I suppose. She's taken a terrible beating.'

My little brother made no mention of Cruikshank's voice. Did it really happen or did I imagine it?

There was no time to go into that now. The most pressing requirement was to get Leila to a place of safety. Giles volunteered to ride back to Dunmere Hall and get the chaise.

'And bring Coggins and Fowler back with you,' I shouted as he made for the door. 'I told them to turn in, so present my apologies and tell them they're needed here . . . And tell them to bring their small kit.'

'Small kit?'

'Soldier talk for an overnight bag — oh, and their pistols, with plenty of powder and shot . . . Well, go on, get a move on!'

I was concerned about my two mercenaries. When all is said and done, they were soldiers, not servants, and both had expressed regret at leaving the army. The prospect of some action should perk them up but I would have to discuss their future seriously with them once the present threat to Leila was over.

I stayed with Emily's friend until she regained consciousness and was able to sip a little water. I then set about righting most of the furniture in order to be able move more easily about in the cottage. Upstairs, I found a fabric bag and filled it with clothing that I thought she would need during her convalescence. I also took the cover from her bed, which, on my return to the kitchen, I placed around her shoulders. The colour was returning to her face and she seemed a little more like her old self.

I then asked her where she had hidden the bag of gold.

'There are only a few guineas left in it,' she said ruefully. 'But I'd be damned if I was

193

going to let Harwood have it! It's in an iron pot in a recess an arm's length up the chimney, on the right-hand side. You'll have to put the fire out first, of course.'

I righted a kitchen chair and helped Leila onto it. She sat bent forward, her elbows resting on her thighs. In this way her wounds didn't come into contact with its upright back. She insisted she was all right so I took the kettle through to the other room and after raking apart the burning wood in the hearth, I doused it with the water. When the smoke and steam had cleared I reached up the chimney and retrieved the pot from its hiding place. Removing the lid I pulled out Harwood's bag and took it back to Leila in the kitchen.

She looked up as I came in. 'It's a nice bag isn't it? I thought of using it as a reticule. You won't find much in it, I'm afraid.'

'There may be more in it than you think, my dear. That scoundrel Harwood wouldn't go to all this trouble for a handful of gold coins.'

It was a drawstring bag made of soft leather with a flat, round, stiffened base. I shook the remaining coins out on the kitchen table. There were a few Spanish Escudos but the rest were gold Louis, about a dozen in all. I then turned the bag inside out and studied the base. 'Just as I thought,' I said. 'There's a slit in the lining.' I worked my fingers between the layers of fabric. 'And there's something tucked inside. A letter perhaps?'

The paper was of good quality. I unfolded it carefully. Whatever it was, it wasn't a letter. The document was headed, *Conduite Sûre*, which my schoolboy French told me, was 'Safe Conduct' and it went on to say, in that language, that Colonel Roland Harwood was an *agent Français*. It bore this year's date and was signed by none other than the Marquis du Quesne, Governor of New France.

'So, the Honourable Roly is in the pay of the French!' I exclaimed. 'No wonder he was so anxious to get his bag back. This piece of paper is more valuable to him than gold. In the wrong hands it could mean his death.'

'Then we must be sure to place it in those hands,' Leila said venomously.

I noticed she was trembling. This was possibly a reaction to the ordeal she had been through or it could simply be that she was feeling cold now the fire was out. There was no point in relighting it as Giles would be back soon with the chaise, so I wrapped the bedcover tighter around her and took the kettle out to the pump to make some tea.

As I was filling the kettle it occurred to me that the gold probably hadn't been won at the tables at all, but was payment for services rendered. But what services, I wondered? Before leaving the Carolinas I'd heard talk of some of the northern colonies banding together for protection from attack by the French. Perhaps Harwood was feeding his paymasters information on the likelihood of the southern colonies joining them, or even taking a more active role by arguing against such an alliance.

I was drinking my second dish of tea when Giles arrived. He looked relieved to see Leila sitting on a chair, and delighted when she smiled at him. 'Right, Tom, ready when you are,' he said cheerfully. 'I say, is there any more tea in the pot?'

'Did you ride back?'

He looked puzzled. 'No, I left the horse at the stable and drove the chaise. I brought Coggins and Fowler just like you said.'

He was quite right. That *is* what I said but it left me with the chaise and a lame horse.

I shouted to the two former soldiers to come in. They shuffled awkwardly into the little kitchen, Fowler letting out a quiet 'Blimey' when he saw Leila's face.

'Are we taking her home with us?' Giles asked innocently.

I pulled a face. 'Mother would love that! No. I still have the keys of the priory so I was planning to take her there, and leave Coggins and Fowler to guard her. That's why they needed their pistols and overnight things, but first I have to get word to Uncle Reuben urgently. Roland Harwood is a French agent and I want his help to apprehend him.'

He whistled in amazement. 'How the devil . . . ?'

'I'll explain on the way. Come on, we're wasting time. You're off to Chester barracks, old son, and we've to go by way of the Hall to get you a horse.'

'Take my horse.' It was Leila.

We were both surprised, and Giles echoed my thoughts when he said, 'You have a horse?'

'How else do you think I get back and forth to the tavern?' she replied.

'My little brother would cut a fine figure riding side-saddle,' I said derisively.

'Who said I ride side-saddle?' Leila scoffed.

This made Fowler laugh, which I silenced with a stern look. Giles went off to fetch the animal and I told the other two to help Leila into the chaise. Coggins surprised me by scooping the big woman up in his arms as if she were a child and carrying her out of the room. A rather subdued Fowler followed with the bag of clothing I'd put together for her and some more blankets and pillows that I told him to fetch from the bedroom.

It was now night and although a full moon shone from an almost cloudless sky I sent Fowler back inside to find materials to make a torch to light our way. When he returned I locked the cottage and waited for Giles to appear with the horse.

It wasn't long before he rode out of the shadows on a fine looking bay mare. I handed him the document that I had found in Harwood's bag. 'Guard this with your life,' I said, 'and give it to Uncle Reuben. No one else, understand?' He nodded and tucked it away securely in the breast pocket of his waistcoat, buttoning his topcoat securely over it. 'You know what Harwood looks like,' I continued, 'so you can give him a description. And you might tactfully suggest he sends the Dragoons to block all the roads out of Byley, particularly those to the port of Liverpool.'

We solemnly shook hands and he urged his horse forward, stopping at the carriage, where, without a word, he took Leila's hand in his and gallantly kissed it before galloping away.

At the brow of the hill he stopped, and with the moon behind him, created a dramatic silhouette by causing his horse to rear up and at the same time waving his hat. It was a performance worthy of applause. I had to hand it to him, when it came to pleasing the ladies my little brother was a natural charmer.

We wrapped Leila in the thick bedcover and Coggins took it upon himself to sit in the back of the chaise with her, with the hood up and a large protective arm around her shoulders. I climbed up onto the driving seat and with Fowler walking on ahead with the torch to light our way, we set off, the carriage swinging on its supporting straps with a motion not unlike that of a sedan chair with the porters walking in step.

Fortunately for our injured passenger, and for our walking torchbearer, it wasn't far from the cottage to the priory. When the old building's imposing façade came into view my attention was immediately attracted to a light that appeared to be shining in one of the tall stained-glass windows of the chapel. At first I dismissed it as the reflection of the moon but as the road to the priory was full of twists and turns and the light was always there no matter from which angle I viewed it I had to conclude that the illumination came from within.

When we were closer to the priory but still within the shelter of the trees I reined the horses in. Fowler turned and looked back enquiringly. I called to him in a hoarse whisper to douse the flames and jumped down to join him.

'What's going on, Major,' he asked.

Thinking of the curate's story of ghostly chanting, I was pleased for once that the superstitious Nolan wasn't with us. 'There's a light in the chapel window,' I said.

'Blimey!'

Big Daniel Coggins appeared at my side. I glanced back at Leila and saw that he had left her cocooned in the extra blankets and had packed all the pillows snugly around her.

'She'll come to no harm,' he growled.

Dropping the horses' reins to the ground, I secured them by rolling a large stone over them. Quickly grasping what I was doing, Coggins and Fowler packed similar rocks fore and aft of the rear wheels, kicking them firmly into place with the toes of their boots.

Fowler grinned. 'There,' he said. 'That ain't going nowhere. I take it we're going to take a look inside?'

'Correct,' I replied. 'But first, I suggest we load and prime our pistols.'

17

The key turned noiselessly in the lock and the big oak door swung open without a sound. I turned to the others and, holding my forefinger to my lips, beckoned to them to follow me inside.

The first thing that struck me was how warm it was. The second was that although the chapel doors were open, the light didn't originate from there but from the candles in the row of wall-mounted sconces that lined the stone flagged passageway. There was something else too, an appetizing smell of roast meat.

With Fowler positioned on the far side with his pistol at the ready, I opened the first door we came to. He went inside quickly with me immediately behind him. 'No one 'ere, Major,' he said disappointedly.

It was a large bedroom. There may be no one there now but the fire was lit and a candle burned on a table next to a four-poster bed.

Suddenly, there were sounds of a scuffle and muffled shouting. Then there was a gunshot followed by silence. Fearing what I would see, I dashed out into the passageway.

A little way further down, by another open door, Daniel Coggins was standing with his back to me, a smoking pistol in his hand and someone lying inert at his feet.

My worst fears seemed to be confirmed. 'My God, Coggins. What have you done?'

The big man turned to face me. 'I had to hit him, Major,' he said defensively. 'He grabbed hold of my pistol.' A lop-sided grin spread across his ugly face. 'He'll be all right. Might have a bit of an 'eadache though.'

The man on the floor groaned and sat up. It was Elias Leech. He felt his chin, cautiously working his jaw from side to side.

'What are you doing here, Leech?' I demanded.

He looked up at me and staggered to his feet. He then stood for a moment, steadying himself with the flat of his hand on the wall. 'Now I've lost my job at the tavern I've got nowhere else to go,' he whined. 'I'm not doing no harm. No one's living here anymore.'

Archie Fowler had joined us and was peering in through the open doorway. ''Ere, this is a kitchen and there's a great big joint of beef on the table. Cor, I couldn't 'arf go a slice of that.'

Seizing this as a way of ingratiating himself, Leech said, 'I've just got it out of the oven.

Go ahead, help yourself.'

The little Cockney needed no further bidding and slipped into the room. Pocketing his pistol, he seized a carving knife and cut off a chunk of beef. 'This is a bit of all right,' he said, with his mouth full. 'You want some, Dan?'

I waved my pistol at the open doorway. 'Why don't we all go in? After you, Mr Leech.'

With the village ne'er-do-well back in the kitchen and his escape route cut off by a closed door with my back against it, I felt a lot easier.

'Perhaps you'll tell me how you come to have a key for the priory,' I began.

'The same way I got that nice bit of sirloin,' he said with a sneer, his old bumptiousness returning. 'I helped myself.'

'Mr Coggins!'

The big man was just finishing the slice of meat Fowler had cut for him. 'Sir!' he said, wiping his greasy chin with the back of a huge hand.

'This, er, gentleman has some things to tell us, but I think he may need some persuasion.'

Coggins gave me one of his lop-sided grins. 'Very good, sir,' he said, wiping his fingers on his thighs as he ambled towards us.

Leech was a big man and although there

wasn't much to choose between the two of them in height, much of Leech's bodyweight was fat whereas Coggins was all muscle.

'I'll ask you again,' I said. 'Where did you get a key for the priory?'

'That's my business,' Leech replied.

I nodded to Coggins who wrapped his mighty arms around Leech and squeezed. Taken by surprise from the rear, Leech was powerless. His face went very red and his eyes looked ready to pop out of their sockets.

'All right! All right!' he croaked. 'You're breaking my bloody ribs!'

I nodded again and Coggins relaxed his grip while still maintaining his hold. For a long moment Leech just hung there sucking air into his lungs, his toes just off the ground.

'I'm waiting,' I said.

'I gave Jed Colclough a hand, didn't I?' he gasped. 'He saw me in the street and he asked me to help him lift the dead priest into his coffin.'

A thought struck me. 'Did he leave you alone with the body?'

Coggins lowered him to the ground. Leech breathed a sigh of relief. 'Yeah,' he said. Then he looked up and stared at me defiantly. 'So I went through his pockets. What good is money to a dead'un, eh?'

'And that's where you found the keys to this place. Tie him up with something, Mr Coggins. I haven't finished with him yet.'

Leaving the thieving Leech in the capable hands of my two worthies, I returned to the bedroom where I stripped the bed and made up the fire. Archie Fowler came in just as I was putting the last log in place.

'That's 'im all secure, Major,' he reported.

I asked what they had done with our prisoner.

'We tied 'is 'ands and feet and sat 'im in the pantry,' he said, adding with a grin, 'That should cool 'im down a bit.'

'How do you feel about handling the chaise?' I asked.

The grin never left his narrow face. 'Me old dad was a carter for the brewery. 'E 'ad me handlin' a pair-in-hand when I was ten.'

'Good! Go and bring it up to the door, and mind you don't jolt our invalid. Then bring all the clean linen in and put it on the bed. I'm going to inspect this makeshift lock-up of yours.'

Coggins was busily carving away at the meat when I entered the kitchen. He hurriedly put the knife down and wiped his lips. 'He's in here, Major,' he said, going to a door at the far end of the room and snapping open the latch.

Leech blinked when the door was opened. He was sitting just inside the tiny, windowless room, his wrists and ankles securely bound and a gag firmly in his mouth.

I checked that the ropes were not unduly tight and he could still breath with the gag in his mouth. 'We'll leave him there until we've got Leila settled,' I said.

Grabbing a small jug from the dresser, I filled it with water from a pitcher standing in the sink. 'Bring her in from the chaise will you? I'll be in the bedroom.'

Fowler was in the process of stuffing pillows into clean pillowcases when I went in. By the amount of blankets on the floor, it would seem he had also brought in all the bedclothes from the chaise, those that were not actually wrapped around Leila that is.

I left the jug of water on the bedside cabinet, together with a cup that I'd also brought from the kitchen. I then turned my attention once more to the fire. The logs I had put on earlier were burning merrily and I was pleased to see that there were still plenty in the big basket standing at the side of the hearth. I was just thinking that there must be a log store somewhere and I must remind my two retainers to look for it in the morning when Coggins came in carrying Leila in his arms.

'Put her on the bed,' I said, 'and you can unwrap her now.'

Free of the bedcover and blankets, Leila was able to stretch her limbs, wincing a little at the twinges of pain induced by the movement. The big man helped her into a sitting position, her head and back resting on a mound of pillows hurriedly put there by Fowler. The two men then painstakingly covered her legs with the bedclothes. I felt I couldn't leave her in better hands, but before I did I had some unsettled business with Elias Leech.

Leaving Leila to rest, I marched Coggins and Fowler back to the kitchen and told them to drag Leech out of the pantry. He looked nervously around the room as Coggins lifted him to his feet and undid the rope around his ankles. I stepped forward and untied the gag. I gave him a few moments to catch his breath before I began to question him.

Since discovering that he'd had the keys to the priory since Cruikshank's funeral, I'd been doing a lot of thinking about Mr Leech. 'So you came to live here after Josh Napper dismissed you, right?' I said.

He stared back at me defiantly. 'What if I did? I had to have somewhere to sleep, and nobody was using the place.'

'You've had a key since Cruikshank's

funeral,' I said conversationally. 'What was to stop you coming here before you were kicked out of the tavern?'

'Nothing, I suppose,' he said, with a sly smile.

I smiled back. 'I bet it was you who frightened that curate, right?'

Leech sniggered. 'What a laugh. You should have seen him run.'

He was more relaxed now, and still smiling, he held out his wrists, as if having them tied was all part of the joke. While he was looking down at his bonds I winked at the others.

'What did you do with Cruikshank's body?' I shouted at him.

That took the smile off his face. In fact, the effect was quite dramatic. He shot up straight. His eyes bulged and the colour drained from his face. I expected a protestation of innocence but he said nothing.

'Mr Coggins!'

The big man grabbed him from behind and Leech squealed in fear as two big, muscular arms wrapped around him and held him in a vice-like grip.

'All right! All right!' he screamed.

I nodded to Coggins who grinned and released his hold.

'I got talking to a one-eyed chap in the tavern,' Leech began. 'Silas his name was.

He'd had a few, and after a while he started telling me about this doctor out Wilmslow way who pays good money for fresh dead'uns. He told me the doctor's name and everything.'

He was sweating profusely so I told him to sit down and sent Fowler to fetch him a drink of water. When the cup was offered to him he took it in both hands and drained it in one draught. He then handed the empty cup back to Fowler with a nod of thanks and carried on with his story.

'This Silas asked me if anyone had died in Goostrey lately. Well, there was Gus Warburton whose horse rolled on him but it didn't seem right to me, digging honest folk up from the graveyard, so I didn't mention him. Then I thought of the Reverend. He had no family. You know that, sir. There was only yourself and Sir Rupert at the funeral — and Mr Hulse of course — and none of you liked him, I heard you say so. So I knew no one would miss him.'

'And you had his keys to the priory.'

'It wasn't as if he had a family like Gus,' Leech said sulkily.

I paced the room for a few minutes thinking of what to do with him. Then I had it!

'Stand him up, Coggins, and turn him to face me,' I said, and with that, I placed a chair behind the kitchen table and sat at it, like a magistrate.

'Mr Leech, by selling information as to the whereabouts of Leila Sculley you have caused that lady undue pain and suffering. It must have been obvious to you that the man seeking her meant her harm, but of course we can't prove that.'

Leech looked at each of us in turn with his shifty eyes, fearful of what was coming next.

'But by your own admission, you are a body snatcher, and we are all witnesses to the fact. Am I right?'

He nodded. 'But you don't get hanged for it, or sent to the colonies. Silas told me.'

'He was right,' I said. 'But if I hand you over to the authorities you *will* get a term of imprisonment, and you won't enjoy that I promise you.'

I've never seen a man look so wretched. Or so relieved when I followed it up with: 'But I am offering you an alternative.'

I do believe if Coggins hadn't prevented him, Leech would have got down on his knees. 'Anything, sir,' he pleaded. 'I've heard about what goes on in prisons.'

After a long pause, I said, 'How would you like to be a soldier?'

That brought him up short and he stood thinking for a moment. Behind him I could see Coggins and Fowler smirking.

Eventually he spoke. 'Thank you Sir Thomas. A soldier's life is hard, I've heard tell, but at least I'll get my food regular — and a roof over my head.'

'Even if it is only made of bleedin' canvas sometimes,' Fowler added with a toothy grin.

'You'll also get a uniform,' I said. 'Just make sure you wear it with honour. And there is one more thing you'll get in the army, Mr Leech. It's something you can't see, but believe me you will feel it, and that's comradeship. I have a feeling you will benefit greatly from the experience. Untie his wrists, Mr Coggins. I'll take him back to Dunmere Hall with me.'

I got up from the table feeling that my father, the magistrate, would have been proud of me.

18

Having first checked that Leila was all right (she was sleeping soundly), I left Coggins on first watch and set off in the chaise with Leech, back to Dunmere Hall.

All men from farming stock are capable of driving a team of horses so, handing him the reins, I travelled sitting in the back with my pistol in my lap, just in case he changed his mind. Neither of us spoke during the short journey. Leech had a lot to think about and so did I.

Sergeant Finch didn't disappoint me. Our head groom was waiting with Hagar in his usual spot on the far side of the bridge over the moat. This time I thought he looked a little the worse for wear.

Telling Leech to stop the chaise, I asked if everything was all right.

Finch gave Leech a puzzled look and then weaved his way across to the carriage and opened the door. He smiled at me; no it wasn't a smile, it was more like a silly grin. 'Welcome home, Sir Thomas,' he said. I caught his breath; it smelled like Josh's brew house.

'Have you been celebrating, Sergeant?'

He put his heels together and stood erect. 'A few drinks in my quarters with a fellow cavalryman, sir,' he reported. 'Colonel Neville sent a Dragoon with a message for Lady Neville, sir. The trooper doesn't have to report back 'til the morning, so we've been swapping tales.'

'About the cavalry?'

'What else, sir?'

'And having a little refreshment too before you turned in.'

Finch grinned. 'Aye, you're right there, sir.'

This was heaven sent. To get word to my uncle about Leech and then wait for him to send an escort could take days. Now I could hand him over to Finch, and the Dragoon would see him safely delivered to the twenty-second.

'Take my place in the carriage, Finch,' I said loudly. 'I think Leech should drive don't you? This brave fellow is going to take the King's shilling, don't y'know.' As I swapped places with my old tutor, I said quietly, 'I want you to keep him somewhere secure tonight, just in case he has a change of heart.' Then in a louder voice, I added, 'He can ride with the trooper when he leaves for Chester in the morning. Fix him up with a horse, will you? Tell the trooper there will also be a letter for Colonel Neville, and he is not to leave without it.'

'So you want me to lock Leech up for the night?' Finch whispered.

I nodded and smiled as I handed him my pistol. 'That's what I like about you, Finch, you're so quick to grasp my meaning.'

★   ★   ★

At breakfast next morning, my mother was astounded when I told her how I'd discovered Roland Harwood's treachery and that I'd sent my little brother to enlist the aid of our uncle in apprehending the scoundrel.

'There are Dragoons at Chester barracks. They could be galloping to Byley Hall at this very minute,' I said.

'But Roland seemed such a charming man.'

'You don't know the half of it, Mother.'

Excusing myself, I left the breakfast table. I was on tenterhooks. What was Harwood planning to do today? He didn't know of my visit to the cottage on the Swettenham road. He had failed in his first attempt to find the moneybag, having no option but to call it a day when Leila passed out. As far as he knew she was still where he and the Cleggs had left her and this morning she would either be

214

dead or recovered sufficiently to be ques-
tioned again. I prayed that the soldiers would
get to Byley Hall before he set off to round
up his villainous gang and make another
attempt.

'You will be back for luncheon,' my mother
called, in such a way that it wasn't so much a
question, more an order.

'I'll do my best,' I replied.

After arranging for Nolan to deliver some
essential supplies to the priory, I went to the
stables, calling for Finch to saddle me a
horse. Perhaps there was a way I could delay
Harwood until the soldiers arrived.

A Dragoon's saddle shabraque draped over
one of the stalls reminded me instantly of the
letter I had yet to pen to my uncle regarding
Elias Leech. I asked Finch if he had writing
utensils in his lodging.

'Of course I have, sir. I'm an educated
man,' he said with mock indignation, adding
with a grin, 'You'll find all you need on the
table by the window, sir, pens, paper, ink,
everything. I've even got some o' that soft,
unsized paper for soaking up the surplus ink.
Much better than the old messy way of
shaking sand over your writing.'

Sergeant Finch's quarters were built over
the stables. He regarded the stable yard
and the buildings surrounding it as his own

private domain and rather liked 'living over the shop' as it were. His rooms were dry and comfortable and benefited from the warmth generated by the animals below. Steps led up to the entrance door, which opened directly into the kitchen, and this is where I found the trooper sitting in his shirtsleeves having his breakfast.

He was a big, handsome fellow, in his forties I'd say, with a rather splendid moustache. He made to stand up as I entered the room but I signalled to him to carry on spooning his porridge.

'Has Sergeant Finch told you about the new recruit?' I asked.

'Indeed he has,' the man replied, wiping his whiskers with his napkin. 'I'll see him safely to Chester barracks, sir, never fear.'

The writing implements were immediately obvious and I sat and wrote the letter to my uncle adding that, in my opinion, a bit of discipline and being taught to have pride in himself and the regiment would bring out the best in Leech.

The Dragoon came into the sitting room to retrieve his coat that was hanging on a hook behind the door.

'I want you to give this letter to Colonel Neville,' I said as I carefully applied the 'blotting' paper. 'It explains why I am sending

Elias Leech back with you.'

'Join the army and be a postman,' the man said with a grin. 'No offence, sir, but that's what brought me here, to deliver a letter *from* the colonel. Well, it wasn't a letter exactly, more an invitation.'

'So, postmen read the messages they are entrusted with, do they?' I said with mock severity.

His face fell. 'Oh, no, sir. I wouldn't do that, sir. The corporal of horse told me what it was when he gave it to me. He said it was an invitation to the Ladies' Night Dinner in the Officers' Mess in a couple of week's time. An invitation from the colonel himself, sir.'

I could quite understand the trooper's NCO emphasising the importance of his assignment by telling him what the missive was and whom it was from.

I folded my letter and sealed it, smiling at him reassuringly as I handed it to him. 'Only joking, soldier. I can see you're a man of honour.'

The Dragoon buckled on his long basket hilted sword and I felt a pang of sadness at having resigned my commission, never again to wear the King's scarlet coat.

I went outside. Finch was checking the girth strap on the saddle of my horse. He heard me coming and looked up. 'All ready for you, sir,' he said cheerfully.

'Will that man be all right with a slippery character like Elias Leech, do you think?' I asked as I mounted.

'Don't you worry about him, sir. He's no fool and I'll give him some tips before he leaves. I knows all the dodges. I've escorted a few deserters back to the regiment in my time.'

Finch slapped the horse's rump, and with Hagar at my side, I took the horse out of the yard at a walk. When we had crossed the bridge over the moat and moved out onto the wide avenue that led to the moor I urged him into a canter.

As I neared the spot where I had discovered my mother picking mushrooms for Edwin Cruikshank's breakfast, I had an awful sense of *déjà vu*, for there was someone else there, another female, kneeling on the grassy bank in just the same way as my mother had done. Hagar ran up to her excitedly. She straightened up and looked in my direction. It was Megan Griffith.

'Well, soldier-boy, we meet again,' she said.

Her usual brash confidence wasn't there. Her face looked strained, as though she was worried about something. I peered into her basket. As well as a strong-looking, long-bladed knife and a bunch of small plants with yellow flowers, there was a single shoe, which I thought rather odd.

'What are you gathering,' I asked, 'dandelions?'

She smiled bleakly. 'Not this time, dear. Those are coltsfoot, to make a cough remedy. I'll sell a lot o'that when autumn really sets in.'

There was something very wrong. I cursed the delay but I couldn't just ride on without finding out what the problem was. I got down from my horse, and then I saw the reason for the shoe in the basket, for her right foot was bound tightly with a strip of cloth and lying next to her on the grass was a long stick, freshly cut from the hedge with part of the bough it grew from still attached so that it resembled an elongated 'T'. It was a crutch.

'You've hurt your ankle,' I said, stating the obvious.

She shrugged resignedly. 'I twisted it in a tree root coming through the wood. Very clumsy of me. It'll be all right. I'll rub it with comfrey oil when I get home.'

Hagar licked her toes. She giggled, and with the aid of the stick, began to stand up. I helped her by supporting her free arm. Once upright, and with the crutch tucked under her arm, she tried taking a step on her injured ankle. 'Oo-argh!' she exclaimed, her face

219

contorted with pain. Quickly shifting her weight to her other foot, she stood panting for a moment. Little beads of perspiration glistened on her forehead.

'I'm sure it didn't hurt that much before I knelt down,' she gasped.

Oh, what the hell! If Uncle Reuben had despatched a troop of Dragoons immediately after Giles made his report, it would be a toss up to see who got to Byley Hall first, me or them. If he hadn't, then Harwood would no doubt now be on his way to Leila's cottage or Clegg's yard anyway. In either case, she was safely out of harm's way at the priory with Coggins and Fowler to guard her.

'It's a long way to your cottage,' I said. 'You can ride on my horse.'

'That's what I like about you, soldier-boy, you're so masterful,' she replied coquettishly, allowing me to lift her in my arms while she located the stirrup iron with her good foot.

She was no lightweight. 'Hurry up,' I gasped. 'Spread you're legs, woman!'

'Fie! Sir Thomas, and me an innocent country lass,' she replied with a laugh. Then, with her foot in the stirrup, she grasped the horse's mane with one hand and the cantle with the other and heaved herself up into the saddle. And there she sat, her skirts hitched up above her knees, her left foot in the stirrup on my side, her injured right foot dangling down on the other, and looking as pleased as punch.

'Pass me the basket,' she said, 'and don't leave that stick behind. It took me ages to cut.'

And so we set off across the moor with me, staff in hand like some biblical prophet, leading the horse with Megan sitting happily on its back, and Hagar running in circles around us.

'I feel somewhat guilty,' Megan said at length.

'Why should you feel guilty?'

'Well, you were obviously on your way somewhere and now you're taking me home.'

I didn't reply immediately, and then, simply because I needed to confide in some-one, and who better than Welsh Meg, a person renowned for keeping her own council, I told her the whole story about Leila, the Cleggs and Harwood.

I concluded with, 'So my journey to Byley Hall was probably unnecessary anyway.'

She laughed until tears ran down her cheeks. 'I'll say it was unnecessary, soldier-boy. If your Colonel Harwood drank the whole bottle of elderflower wine I gave Leila Sculley then he's probably still squatting in his closet.'

I was puzzled. 'Was there something wrong with your wine?'

'I'll have you know there's nothing wrong with my wine' she said, pretending to be offended. 'It's what I laced it with . . .

'I've never had a rival before so I decided to teach Mistress Sculley a lesson. I added a little Buckthorn to the wine. Buckthorn is a strong purgative. One glass would give you the runs for a week. God knows what a whole bottle would do to you!

'Anyway, from what you've told me it sounds like he deserved whatever he got.'

19

Megan Griffith's cottage stood on its own on the outskirts of Goostrey. I tied up the horse and carried her inside, laying her gently on her bed.

'Aren't you going to join me?' she said, a mischievous twinkle in her eye.

I affected an injured look. 'Madam. A gentleman would never take advantage of an injured lady,' I said, imitating an actor's exaggerated way of speaking.

'Go then! Leave me if you must,' she cried, copying me, and then, in her normal voice, adding, 'Just make sure that stick's within reach, will you? Oh, and soldier-boy . . . ' She held out her hand.

'Yes,' I replied, taking it in mine.

'Thank you.'

I bent down and kissed her on the forehead. Megan was an exceedingly handsome woman and it was strange that I never felt tongue-tied or awkward in her company. Perhaps she was a witch after all.

As with Leila, before I left my second invalid I made sure she had fresh water, brought in some logs for the fire and checked that she had food in the pantry. I had no qualms about leaving her on her own. Welsh Meg was more than capable of taking care of herself and there was no fear of thieves or robbers troubling her, for apart from a nervous maiden seeking a love potion or a farmer wanting a decoction to ward off the cowpox, most local folk gave her cottage a wide berth. Being thought to possess the evil eye was more effective than having the fiercest of guard dogs. I'd call back in a day or so though, just to check.

In spite of my promise to my mother that I would try to be home for luncheon, I made a small detour and called in at Josh Napper's tavern. Old Simon met me in the stable yard. He showed no pleasure in seeing me, which disappointed me rather.

Josh's ill-tempered ostler never smiled at anyone, but having been the bearer of good news about his job, I thought he might at least have acknowledged my arrival with a kindly word. Perhaps he didn't really want his old position back.

'Got no hay,' he grumbled. 'Always the same after market day at Beartown. Them drovers' horses eats my hay as though they hasn't been fed for days.'

Although I'd heard the name many times, I had no idea why the local people called

Congleton 'Beartown', and in an attempt to lighten Simon's mood, I asked him if he knew.

'Been called Beartown since good Queen Bess's day,' he said. 'The story goes that holiday time were drawing near, and just when everyone was looking forward to havin' a good old time, a'drinkin' and a'gamblin' while they's a'watching the bear bating, sir, the Congleton bear, it goes and dies!' He leaned forward, lowering his voice conspiratorially. 'D'you know what they did, the good folk of the town what had been saving for months to buy a new bible for the church?'

I could guess but I didn't want to spoil his story so I shook my head.

'They used the money to buy a new bear instead, that's what they did,' he said.

He then made a noise that sounded like a wheezing cough, which was, I suppose, the nearest old Simon could get to a laugh. Well, at least I left him happier than I found him.

★ ★ ★

Whether people call their midday meal dinner or lunch is not so much a class thing; it's really when they actually have the main meal of the day. At Dunmere Hall we have a hearty breakfast, a light meal, our luncheon, at midday and at least a three- or four-course meal, our dinner, in the evening. Working folk mostly have their main meal, their dinner, in the middle of the day and a light supper in the evening. So, to Josh's customers this was dinner time, and the taproom was full of folk, tobacco smoke and noise.

There were a few faces I recognised but the rest, I assumed, were people on their way home from market. Josh was where I expected to see him, weaving between the tables with both fists full of foaming tankards, and Emily was at the long table in front of the barrels, pouring beer for eager customers from the big jug.

There were a couple of noisy young bloods at the table who, to me, seemed a little too eager, but Emily was well used to this and more than capable of holding her own when it came to exchanging good-natured banter.

I pushed my way through the crush. What I had to say would undoubtedly take the smile off her face but I had to do it. At least I could reassure her that Leila was in safe hands.

The lads in front of me were served and I moved forward just as Emily turned to fill her jug from one of the barrels.

'Thomas!' she exclaimed, when she turned back and saw me standing there, grinning at her. Quickly getting over her surprise she added, 'A tankard of ale is it?'

And, grinning like the tongue-tied fool I was, I nodded briskly. Then Josh came back, and at the same time Milly Goodrich appeared from the kitchen with a tray of clean tankards. Leaving Milly to dispense the ale, I took Josh and Emily to one side and gave them a condensed version of what had happened to Leila.

'I'd be the first to call for Harwood's execution,' Josh said when I'd finished. 'But I'd give him a quicker and cleaner death than the law prescribes.'

'What's that, Papa?' Emily asked innocently.

Josh stared straight ahead. 'A traitor gets hung, drawn and quartered, girl.'

Emily shuddered. I wanted to put my arm around her but her father beat me to it. She looked at me with those incredibly big brown eyes. 'And Leila is all right?' she asked anxiously.

'She's been badly beaten but there were no bones broken,' I replied. 'Given time and care, she'll soon be up and about again.'

Josh surprised me by suddenly grinning at me. 'I'd love to be a fly on the wall at Chester barracks when that work-shy rascal Elias Leech gets there,' he said.

I smiled back at him. 'I thought it would do

him some good, develop his character.'

'It'll develop something, even if it's only blisters on his feet from all that marching,' he said laughing. His mirth was short-lived however and his face darkened. 'The Cleggs!' he hissed. 'What are we going to do about the Cleggs?'

I was ready for that. 'I'll file charges with the magistrate and he'll send the Constable to arrest them.'

Josh looked thoughtful. 'That'll cost you a bit, Sir Thomas. Willy Dalton don't come cheap and he'll have to recruit a lot of help. You'll have to pay for that as well.'

'I don't care what it costs. I just want them locked up,' I said. My anger was making me talk loudly and I was conscious of a few heads turning in my direction.

'Are you staying for dinner?' Emily suddenly asked brightly.

I was sorely tempted. Had it been possible for Emily and I to have a meal together, I wouldn't hesitate, but I knew she was needed to fill tankards. To sit and gaze at my love through the smoky haze of the taproom whilst spooning down Josh's lamb stew would be a poor substitute. So I supposed I'd have to go home and please Mother.

Then I suddenly had a bright idea. 'No,' I said. 'But why don't you come and dine with me this evening, at the Hall? I'll send a carriage for you about half past seven . . . That's if it's all right with your father?'

Josh beamed. 'Of course it's all right, Sir Thomas. You go and enjoy yourself, my girl. Milly and me will manage. Without Leila here singing her songs, we'll be quiet this evening anyway.'

I left the tavern feeling rather pleased with myself. Giles was waiting for me when I got back to the Hall. My news about Emily coming to dinner was received with scepticism.

'Don't you think you should have asked Mamma first?' he said.

'I can invite who I like to dinner in my own home,' I replied firmly and with more confidence than I felt.

Giles decided to change the subject. 'I say, that Safe Conduct certainly got things moving at the barracks,' he said excitedly. 'I told Uncle Reuben what you said about the Dragoons.'

'You really must stop calling him that,' I said. 'He'll soon be your commanding officer.'

'Yes, yes, I know. Anyway, without more ado, he sent for their officer in charge. I think the poor chap had gone to bed. When he did eventually put in an appearance I was politely dismissed, so I didn't hear what 'the colonel' actually said to him, but whatever it was, it wasn't long before a corporal of horse and four troopers were galloping off to Byley. I hope they got there before Harwood decided to leave. Uncle Reuben said nabbing a spy would be a feather in the cap for everyone . . . I say, Tom, d'you think I'll get a mention in dispatches?'

I looked at Giles's eager young face and I had to smile. 'I would think that very likely,' I said, 'and something of an achievement, considering you haven't taken up your commission yet . . . Oh, and don't worry about Harwood not being at Byley Hall when the Dragoons get there. I have it on good authority that he most certainly will.'

Suddenly my little brother looked troubled. 'D'you know, in a way I was hoping he wouldn't be,' he said. 'I've arranged to take Prudence out this afternoon and, well, you know ladies. If it comes out that I'm the one responsible for the brutal and licentious soldiery bursting into her home and dragging off their house guest, she probably won't want anything more to do with me.'

'I don't pretend to know the ladies as well as you, little brother, but the way that young lady was looking at you yesterday I don't think you've got anything to worry about.

And when she discovers the part you played in the apprehension of a dangerous spy, you'll be a hero.'

'What's that? Who's a hero?' said my mother appearing at the doorway.

'Oh, just Tom talking nonsense, as usual,' Giles replied with a laugh. Then, still in a mischievous mood, he added, 'I say, Mamma. Tom's invited a young lady to dinner.'

A ghost of a smile hovered on my mother's lips. 'And would that be the lovely Prudence Bottomley?' she asked teasingly.

I took a deep breath. 'No, Mother. It's Emily Napper. Joshua Napper's daughter.'

She couldn't have looked more startled if the Devil himself had leapt out of the fireplace. 'That serving wench!' she screeched. 'I'll not have her at *my* table.'

'But she's my friend,' I protested. 'Surely I can invite a friend to my own house.'

My mother looked at me coldly. 'But it's *not* your house, Thomas. And if you continue to flaunt convention, it never will be.'

And with that she swept out of the room.

Giles looked at me sheepishly. 'I say, Tom, I'm sorry about that. I didn't think Mamma would take it so badly.'

'I would've told her myself this afternoon anyway,' I said with a sigh. 'And I'm sure her reaction would have been just the same. You brought it forward an hour or so, that's all.'

I was about to say more when I heard someone ride into the courtyard, the sound of hooves being followed by a loud hammering at the door. The urgency of the sound caused both Giles and I to make for the entrance hall but Smallwood beat us to the door.

The visitor was Nolan, out of breath from his gallop. 'Come quickly, sir,' he gasped, as soon as the door was opened. 'There are six of them attacking the priory. Coggins and Fowler are holding them off but they've got muskets.'

'The Cleggs,' I said. 'Smallwood! Tell Finch to saddle my horse, and keep Hagar with you; I don't want her getting shot . . . And Nolan! In a situation like this I think swords are called for. Mine's in my bedroom, but there are more in the gatehouse. Go and chose one for yourself.'

'Tell Finch to saddle my horse as well, Smallwood,' Giles shouted to the retreating butler, following this with: 'Hang on Nolan, I'll come with you.'

After buckling on my sword and priming and loading the pistol I always carried in a holster on my saddle, I hurried outside to join the other two. I found them standing outside the gatehouse. Giles was making a hole in his newly acquired sword belt with the tip of his knife and Nolan was stroking his horse's nose. All we needed now was Finch with the other two. It wasn't long before our head groom appeared. I was surprised to see him leading two horses and riding a third himself. He was wearing a padded leather coat, and when he got nearer I saw he had buckled on his old cavalry sword.

'From what Smallwood told me, sir, it sounded like you were forming a small troop of mounted militia. I'll come along, if that's all right.'

'You're most welcome, Finch,' I said, heaving myself into the saddle. 'As a mere infantryman, I'll be most grateful for your expert knowledge.'

Giles sat on his horse grinning broadly. 'Well, counting Coggins and Fowler, that makes six of us,' he said gleefully. 'The odds are even now.'

'The odds are always in the favour of the righteous,' I shouted. 'Never forget that. Come, gentlemen. Let's go!'

20

We could hear the sound of gunfire long before we got to the priory, evidence that the Cleggs knew I'd moved Leila there but didn't know that their paymaster had been arrested.

When we reached the trees I quietly gave the order to dismount, and telling the others to stay with the horses, I made my way forward cautiously on foot until I could see the combatants. Shots were still being exchanged, a desultory crackle from the trees to my right being answered by an occasional puff of smoke at the priory windows. By the sound of it the Cleggs had muskets, and certainly more than one, whereas my men were armed only with pistols.

I studied the scene. Were I Abraham Clegg, I would divide my muskets, and then, under the cover of fire, I would send half my men sprinting across the open space to the priory wall. They could then attack the defenders from two sides.

These were not soldiers but surely they knew that the range of a pistol was only a quarter of that of a musket. Perhaps the Cleggs didn't know it was only pistols returning their fire. Perhaps they couldn't tell the difference in the sound. In any event, something would have to happen soon to end this stalemate. Dwindling ammunition would force the Cleggs to either press home their attack or give up, depending on what Harwood had promised to pay them; or, worse still, out of sheer frustration, Daniel Coggins would rush out and attack *them*.

I crept back to where the others were waiting with the horses.

When he saw me, Finch's eyes glinted with excitement. 'Are we going to charge them, sir?' he asked hopefully.

'I'm sorry to disappoint you, old friend, but there would be no glory in it. They'd simply run away into the trees. No, the only way to winkle them out is to creep up behind them.'

'That's a splendid idea,' Giles said eagerly. 'Let's go.'

'Not so fast, little brother. This is a job for pistols, not swords. Do you have a pistol?'

'You know I haven't,' he said petulantly. 'You told us to bring swords.'

'A good cavalryman always carries a pistol in a holster on his saddle. Just look at Finch's horse. He has one like mine.'

My old teacher smiled. 'You mean *you* have one like mine, sir,' he said gently.

'Nolan doesn't have one on his horse's

saddle!' Giles exclaimed triumphantly.

'I'm sorry chum. He always carries a pistol in his pocket.' And turning to my valet, I asked, 'Am I right, Nolan?'

Giving Giles an apologetic look, the sturdy little Irishman fished deep into the capacious pocket in his knee-length coat and drew out his weapon.

'And being an infantryman, he knows how to move noiselessly through wooded county,' I added.

'But Finch was in the cavalry!'

'Who do you think taught me how to stalk a deer?'

Giles shrugged resignedly. 'Someone has to stay with the horses, I suppose,' he said sportingly, taking out his pipe.

As we set off, I saw Finch pat him on he shoulder and hand him his tobacco pouch.

With our pistols loaded and cocked, we progressed slowly through the wood, placing each foot with care so as not to snap a twig or making any sudden movement that would panic the birds resting in the branches above us and give away our position. As we got closer to the spot where I had seen the Cleggs I signalled to the others to spread out.

We were about fifty feet away when I eventually saw them, standing at the edge of the spinney. There seemed to be only two of them. They had their backs to us and were looking at the priory. One was a big fellow, the other much smaller. I didn't think the Cleggs had any small men in their family. They seemed to be talking, and yes, they were smoking. Obviously they had twigged that the defenders were only using pistols and had worked out the range, as they were making no attempt to take cover. Were they goading the defenders, I wondered? Another yard and I recognised them; my God! It was Coggins and Fowler!

Leaving caution aside I strode towards them. Fowler spun round, his pistol pointing straight at me.

'Hold your fire,' I shouted. 'It's me, with Nolan and Finch.'

'Blimey, Major,' he said, with a toothy grin. 'I thought you was those villains coming back.'

Finch and Nolan joined me and there was much handshaking and backslapping.

'So what happened to the Cleggs?' I asked.

Coggins shrugged. 'We wasn't doing any good with our pistols at that range so we sneaked out the back way to get closer, going through the trees like you were doing just now.'

'We could've gone right up to 'em and tapped 'em on the shoulder,' Fowler added gleefully.

The big man regarded his small friend proudly. 'But Archie shot their leader and the others ran away.'

He stepped aside, and there, lying where it had fallen, half hidden by brambles, was the body of Abraham Clegg. As I stood looking down at the bully's twisted form, Cruikshank's voice came back to me: *Abraham Clegg is a dead man walking.*

Archie Fowler brought me back to the present. 'Well, Major, you always said to shoot the ones giving the orders,' he said defensively.

The matter would have to be reported to the magistrate and Clegg's body taken back to Goostrey.

'Right!' I said. 'Coggins, get him out of that bush. You help him, Fowler — and you, Nolan. And Finch, you ride back to the Hall and fetch the Estate Wagon — and tell Giles to bring the horses up here. Well, go on then, what are you waiting for?'

With muttered curses as the brambles snagged their clothes and scratched their hands, the three former soldiers dragged Abraham Clegg out of the bushes.

Giles arrived with the horses as they were laying him on the wide strip of grass that separated the priory from the belt of trees. 'Well, that's one less,' he said, with cheerful lack of sympathy. 'Finch said the others ran away. Are we going after them?'

'No, I'll leave them to the Constable. I'm going to Sir Henry Leyton's now, d'you want to come?'

Sir Henry had taken over when my father resigned as the local Justice of the Peace. He was an old friend of the family, a little man with a booming voice and an equally loud laugh. In spite of his small stature, you always knew when Sir Henry was present at a function. But for all that, he was a just and honest man with a genuine desire to improve the common good. With the Cleggs' reputation, I had no doubt he would accept Abraham Clegg's death as self-defence and readily issue a warrant for the arrest of his sons.

'Prudence will have given me up by now, so I'll stay with Leila for a while if that's all right?' Giles replied philosophically.

'Perfectly. I think it's unlikely the Cleggs will come back, but I'll leave Coggins and Fowler here with you just in case. I'll also leave Nolan to wait for Finch and the wagon. Tell him he's to go with Finch to Jed Colclough's. I'll call in at Colclough's workshop on my way to Leyton House and warn him to expect Abraham Clegg's corpse.'

I mounted my horse and set off across the same strip of turf where I had seen my mother, with flowers in her hair like a shepherdess in one of Antoine Watteau's romantic paintings, dancing barefoot while Edwin Cruikshank played a panpipe. In a fit of anger, I had aimed my fowling piece at the rogue priest but changed my mind at the last moment and blasted a crow out of the sky instead. How long ago that all seemed, and how different things would be now if I hadn't altered my aim.

Out on the moor there was a scattering of bedraggled sheep nibbling at the stunted grass and a hawk hovering above a clump of gorse, but apart from that I was quite alone.

I was still thinking about my mother, and in particular her reaction to me inviting Emily to dinner at Dunmere Hall. She was right, of course, there *was* a big gulf between an innkeeper's daughter and someone born into the gentry — and a knight of the realm at that! But why should that be? Emily had classical good looks, spoke nicely, dressed well and her manners were impeccable. She could converse on almost any subject and, if she could run a busy tavern, running a large house would be child's play. She was possibly more intelligent and certainly had more character than any of the eligible young ladies in our circle of friends and acquaintances but, because of her roots, she would never be accepted in polite society. How the devil could I change that?

Riding through the countryside on a fine English day, with the sun on my back and the air smelling like wine, it was easy to think thoughts of love.

It seemed as though I'd known Emily all my life. I remember her arriving in the village with Josh. I was eleven at the time, four years older than her. With her coffee-coloured complexion and huge brown eyes, she fascinated me. As I grew older, with burgeoning adolescence fascination became desire and at every opportunity, I would go to Goostrey in the hope of catching a glimpse of her. We would exchange a smile and perhaps a little polite conversation, but nothing more. That is until one evening when I was riding home, a newly-promoted lieutenant on leave from his regiment.

It had been a long, tiring journey from Chester and I decided to stop for some refreshment at Josh Napper's tavern. When I rode into the stable yard, there was no sign of old Simon, so I dismounted and was in the process of undoing my saddle girth when I heard hurried footsteps behind me. It was Emily.

'Oh, Thomas, it's you,' she said, breath-lessly. 'Simon's not at work today, so Father has asked me to look after the horses.'

She smiled at me and I was struck by how lovely she looked in the lamplight.

'Is there anything you don't do around here?' I asked.

'He won't let me help him brew ale,' she said seriously, and then she laughed.

I laughed too. It felt good just to be with her. Then I did something I had wanted to do for a long time, I kissed her. To my delight she responded eagerly. She was soft and warm with a friendly puppy-dog smell, so unlike the stiff and starchy, lavender-scented young ladies I was expected to partner at the Hunt ball. I was transported to heaven, but then, quite unexpectedly, she pushed me away.

'Dear, sweet Tom,' she whispered. 'This will never do. We live in different worlds you and I. To let our feelings run away with us, it will only bring heartache.'

I had looked into her honest brown face and known I was hopelessly in love with her, and in spite of her brief, tragic *affaire* with Edwin Cruikshank, I still felt the same now. That handsome, arrogant bastard had bewitched her, just as he had bewitched my mother and, no doubt, many others beside. But what she had said on that most memorable of all memorable occasions, about us living in different worlds, was all too true and my mother had reminded me just how far apart those worlds were.

A fat hen pheasant suddenly running across the lane in front of my horse brought me back to earth. I steadied my horse then urged him into a canter. I didn't have time to waste on daydreams.

Jed Colclough was attending to a customer when I arrived at his workshop — that is if you can call a dead body a customer. I peered into the coffin and found myself looking at Jimmy Hales the shepherd, a small, white-haired man with a face as brown as a walnut. He looked serene but somewhat unnatural, dressed as he was in his Sunday best clothes. Whenever I'd seen him he'd been wearing a battered old hat and a smock or the 'round frock' over his trousers and shirt as some folk still called the practical garment worn by most countrymen.

I said as much to Colclough.

'I knows just what you mean, Sir Thomas,' he said. 'Jimmy hardly ever went to church you see, and because of that, his wife got into quite a state when he died, saying he wouldn't be allowed into heaven because of his poor attendance record.' He smiled. 'I pacified her by showin' her this,' he said, and pointed to a clump of sheep's wool gripped in the deceased's right hand. 'I told her that when Jimmy's Maker sees this, he'll know he were a shepherd and let him in. The Lord's a shepherd Hisself an' He knows a good shepherd allus has to be with his flock.'

It was a touching story and I congratulated Colclough on his ingenuity.

'Oh, I didn't make it up, sir,' he said with a grin. 'That's an old 'un, that is. I learnt it from my dad . . . Now, Sir Thomas. What can I do for you?'

He raised his eyebrows when I told him about Abraham Clegg but I could see he wasn't surprised to learn of the bully's untimely demise.

'I allus knew he'd come to a bad end,' he said sagely. 'A bad lot them Cleggs; all on 'em. Don't worry about a thing, Sir Thomas. As you're payin', I'll get on with makin' the coffin as soon as Mr Finch gets here with the body. I'll 'ave a word with the vicar as well if you like, ask him to go round and see Mistress Clegg to arrange the funeral.'

'Good idea, Colclough. Tell her I'll see to all expenses. But tell the vicar not to be in too much of a hurry to go round to the Cleggs' place. I'm on my way to see Sir Henry Leyton, to swear out a warrant for the arrest of Abraham's sons. I think it would be better if the Reverend left things for a day or two.'

Colclough touched the side of his nose with his forefinger and winked conspiratorially. 'I takes your meanin', Sir Thomas. Better all round for him to call when them ruffians is all out of the way, eh?' Then he frowned, and it was as if a shadow had passed across his lean, honest face. 'What d'you think will happen to 'em?' he asked with genuine concern.

'I'll recommend transportation,' I said. 'They need strong young men in the colonies. Far better to send the young Cleggs to help build a new country than to the gallows.'

He smiled. 'You're a fair-minded man, Sir Thomas. Just like your father . . . And don't you worry about Abraham. I'll put him in my woodshed. Bein' under the trees it's nice and cool in there. He'll keep for days in there he will.'

21

Sir Henry Leyton greeted me with the news that my uncle had sent a galloper with a dispatch advising him of the evidence he had against Roland Harwood and asking for his approval of the action he was taking to apprehend him.

'I had no hesitation in sending the trooper back with a warrant for Harwood's arrest,' he said decisively.

He asked me if I would like to partake in afternoon tea and when I declined he took me through to his study and there he painstakingly wrote down my testimony regarding the Cleggs' involvement with Harwood, muttering 'shameful' and 'disgraceful' as I told him about Leila Scully's whipping and the ransacking of her cottage. I concluded with a description of the armed siege of the priory and the killing of Abraham Clegg, stating that I was prepared to stand up in court, if necessary, and say I saw the Cleggs firing their muskets at the windows of the building.

'Damned fellow got what he deserved,' he said. 'Tell your man he's nothing to answer for . . . You'll want me to arrest the sons no doubt?'

I said I did, and I agreed to pay whatever costs were necessary, adding: 'Provided you put in a recommendation for the boys to be transported.'

Sir Henry nodded his head. 'Very sensible. The New World is just the place for young men with a surplus of energy.' He put down his pen, took a deep breath, closed his eyes and sighed contentedly. 'Just think. I'll get a bit of peace for a while. No brawling outside the tavern on a Saturday night, and no farmers whingeing about their livestock being stolen . . . How long do you think it will be until another family like the Cleggs come along?'

I shook my head with a smile. I took a glass of sherry with the magistrate, signed the necessary paperwork, and left with his thanks ringing in my ears.

★ ★ ★

Sergeant Finch was waiting for me when I got back to the Hall. He was standing in his usual spot on the far side of the moat bridge with Hagar sitting at his side, her pointed face moving up and down as her gaze alternated between eagerly monitoring my approach and looking up expectantly at Finch. Finally he said something to her, and then she was off, scampering across the bridge, letting out little yelps of pleasure until she met up with me, whereupon she happily trotted alongside my horse until I brought him to a halt.

'You're a good friend of Joshua Napper, are you not Finch?' I said, as I slid out of the saddle.

He looked puzzled. 'Indeed I am, sir.'

'Has he ever talked about his life before he came to Goostrey?'

Finch relieved me of the horse's reins and fumbled in his waistcoat pocket for his stubby brown pipe, which he proceeded to fill with tobacco. 'He comes from Derbyshire, I know that much, sir. There were an outbreak of plague in his village, nothing as bad as the Black Death you understand, but bad enough for Josh. It took both his wife and his livelihood from him.'

I knew Josh had arrived in Goostrey, a penniless widower with his daughter, but I was interested to know what his occupation had been in Derbyshire, so I asked.

Finch got behind the horse where he was sheltered from the wind and applied his tinderbox to his pipe, sucking at the stem until the tobacco in its bowl was ignited.

'His father was a farmer,' he began after expelling a great cloud of smoke. 'So Josh started out working for his dad. Now, I don't know if his family didn't approve of his choice of a wife or he just decided to try something different, but after he got married he got a job with the local innkeeper. He liked that work. That's where he learned how to make ale.'

'You said he lost his livelihood. Did the innkeeper die from the plague too?'

'Oh, no, sir. He didn't die but he sided with the others who said they should be like Eyam and shut themselves off until the outbreak burnt itself out.'

Everyone in this part of the country knew the tragic tale of how, in 1665, the Derbyshire village of Eyam was ravaged by a great plague after a tailor received some infected cloth from London. The good people of Eyam elected to stay within the confines of the village so that the sickness should not spread.

'A very unselfish gesture,' I said.

'Aye, but did you know, sir, that in Eyam, out of a population of 350, over 250 died! Josh was having none of that. He had an uncle who was one of your father's tenant farmers so he buried his wife and walked here with little Emily to find work.'

'His wife, Finch. What do you know about his wife?'

The old cavalryman sucked on his pipe for a long moment. 'I never met her, you understand?' he said. 'But Josh told me she was kind and thoughtful, attentive to his

249

every need, modest and, oh yes, beautiful, not just good-looking or pretty or anything like that, but truly beautiful. As black as your hat, but beautiful.'

Because of Emily's colouring, her delicate features and her polite gentleness, I had assumed her mother was Indian. Josh's list of her attributes seemed to confirm that. 'Where did they meet?' I asked.

'She was a servant in the big house where Josh's father was tenant of the home farm.'

I could see Finch was becoming uneasy with me quizzing him about his friend. 'Just one last question, Finch, then you can get back to the stables. Where was she from?'

'You really should ask Josh, sir,' he said. 'All I know is the master of the house had a very profitable seam of coal on his land and he used a lot of the profits from that to go on exploring trips. Anyway, he brought Emily's mother back with him from one of his journeys, as a companion for his wife, a bit of a novelty like.'

'But where *from*, Finch?'

He smiled and shook his head. 'You really will have to ask Josh that one, Master Thomas.'

As Emily's mother was nothing more than a servant, knowing where she came from wouldn't help me get my love accepted into society, but I was interested nonetheless. And

I had somehow to tell her dinner at the Hall was off. I wasn't looking forward to that!

'I shall, Finch, I shall. Saddle a fresh horse and bring it to the courtyard in half an hour.'

* * *

Full of foreboding, I rode into the tavern yard. Old Simon shuffled out to meet me. Believing that a smile begets a smile, I was about to remark on the fine weather we were having when he forestalled me by grumbling, 'Autumn's on its way, Sir Thomas. I can feel it in me bones. I hates the cold and the damp. It plays the very devil wi' me joints, it does.'

I gave up, and leaving the old curmudgeon to enjoy the prospect of aches and pains to come, I went in search of Josh. I was nearing the door to the taproom when I was brought to a stop by a shout of, 'Belay there!'

A barrel rolled across my path followed by a grinning Joshua Napper. 'Sorry about that, Sir Thomas. Once these things gets a'rolling there's no stopping 'em until they hits the doorstep.'

I was intrigued. 'How do you get it through the door?'

'You has to tip it on its end.'

'I'll give you a hand,' I said, not realizing just how heavy a full barrel of ale was.

But Josh waved me aside. He had the knack of doing it and the barrel was soon positioned in front of the doorway where he had a small cart waiting. Once it was lying on the cart, it was an easy job to wheel it through the tap-room.

Apart from a couple of old, smock-clad locals the room was empty. I would have to search for Emily, I thought, but as I had Josh to myself for a moment I decided to take the plunge and ask him about his wife. Although I knew the answer, I began by asking him how they met.

With the barrel on its side, Josh was busy knocking out the bung and replacing it with a tap. He didn't look up. 'Every mornin'' I delivered milk to the house where she were living,' he said, somewhat defensively. 'I was working on my father's farm then.'

He allowed me to hold the cart steady while he set the barrel back on its end. 'You know I admire your daughter greatly, don't you Napper?' I said.

'I do that, sir,' he replied, grunting as he struggled to position the barrel in line with the others behind the long table.

'Then you will know I mean no offence when I say that it's obvious her mother wasn't European.'

He stood up, wiping the sweat from his

forehead with the hem of his apron. 'It don't matter to me that she wasn't, sir. My darling Ayana was a Princess among women. A more sweeter, gentler soul . . . '

I interrupted him. 'Emily's delicate features and her gentle, well-mannered ways suggest to me that her mother came from the Indian subcontinent,' I said, still fishing for information.

'Then you'd be wrong, sir. She were Abyssinian . . . And if you've come to see Emily, she ain't here. She's gone to market.' Then he grinned. 'Gone to buy pretty ribbons and the like I've no doubt,' he added with a wink. 'She'll be back well before half seven though . . . Now can I get you something, Sir Thomas? Would you care to sample some porter I just got in from Manchester? It's not a patch on the stuff we had in London, I think it must be something to do with the water, but it's a good satisfying drink all the same.'

In a way I was relieved that Emily wasn't there. I had no idea what I was going to say to her. I'd probably get tongue-tied and botch it anyway, I usually did. I declined Josh's offer of a drink and rode away feeling pretty wretched.

But I knew I was doing the wrong thing. Emily had to be told and the longer I left it, the harder it was going to be. By the time I reached the moor I'd made up my mind to go back and wait for her. I was about to turn my horse's head when I suddenly felt an overwhelming compulsion to go to the priory. Something was wrong. I spurred my mount into a gallop and headed for the castellated tower beyond the trees.

All was quiet when I got there. Coggins and Fowler were lounging by the door smoking their pipes and looking very relaxed. The grass deadened the sound of my horse's hooves so I was able to get quite close before they knew of my presence.

But not that close! They both sprung round to face me, pistols at the ready.

'Congratulations, gentlemen. As vigilant as ever, I see. But there's no need to stand guard outside. I grant you it's a fine sunny morning but it is a bit nippy . . . Or is it that Leila objects to you smoking indoors?'

'Nah! Nuffin' like that, Major, and we knows 'ow to wrap up on sentry go, don't we Dan?' Fowler answered chirpily. 'Back in India the lads took to buyin' them *pai jamahs* in the native market. You know, Major, them loose trousers the Muslims wear. We'd wear 'em in bed, a lot warmer than a nightshirt they was, and we'd wear 'em under our breeches when we was on night guard to keep us warm. Dan an' me is wearin' 'em now.'

'She's got a visitor. A fine-looking woman,' Coggins interjected, nodding sagely.

Fowler frowned at his companion. 'They was talking, Major, you know, chattin' and laughing like, and we seemed to be the butt of their jokes — so we left 'em to it.'

Emily! I slid off my saddle and dashed inside. I could hear voices and laughter coming from the bedroom. The door was open. I quickened my step.

The sight that greeted me was not what I had anticipated. I expected to see Leila sitting up in bed, and she was, but the person sitting *on* the bed engaging her in animated conversation was not Emily but Megan Griffith!

Welsh Meg turned her head and smiled at me. 'Hello, soldier-boy,' she purred.

'What the deuce are you doing here?' I exclaimed. I was probably being overly harsh but Megan was the very last person I thought to see laughing and joking with Leila.

She affected a hurt look. 'I brought some marigold salve for the poor girl's wounds,' she said with a pout, and turning to the invalid, said, 'We were just discovering how much we have in common, weren't we Leila?'

It was Leila's turn to smile at me. 'When I'm on my feet again, Megan and I are going to join forces. We are agreed that there is more to be gained by working together than competing with each other.'

The last thing I wanted was to be drawn into a conversation about the type of work these indomitable women had in mind, although I had a feeling it had nothing to do with being on one's feet.

'The last time I saw you, you couldn't bear to stand on your right foot,' I said, in an attempt to cover up my rather rude outburst on finding her there. 'Am I to take it your ankle is less painful now?'

'The oil worked wonders,' Megan replied, 'but I still can't put my weight on it for long periods. I was lucky. I caught Will Gregory, the wagoner, just as he was setting off for Congleton. He brought me here.'

'You've still got to get back.'

She got to her feet aided by a conventional walking stick. 'It's better to be born lucky than rich,' she said huskily, giving me one of her alluring smiles. 'I promised Leila some camomile tea so I'll go and put the kettle on.' I was about to offer to do it for her when she said, 'No, Leila has something troubling her that she says only you can help her with. I'll leave you to talk in private.'

'I have a problem,' Leila whispered as soon as we were alone. 'Immediately I knew who you were I disliked you. No, it was more than that, I hated you.'

I was astounded. 'What on earth have I done to make you feel like that?'

Her face was a mask of desperate bewilderment. It was a look I'd seen before, on the tortured face of Tobias Bloom.

'That's just it,' she said. 'You haven't done anything. In fact I have every reason to like you, but as soon as I was aware you were the son of Sir Rupert Neville I found myself looking for faults, waiting for you to do something that I could pounce on to justify this feeling of antagonism.' She smiled self-consciously. 'You have been kindness itself, Sir Thomas. I just wanted to thank you, and to apologise if this unwarranted ill will I've been harbouring has been apparent in any way.'

Then her eyes began to shine with that strange, unearthly light I'd witnessed before, and the voice of Edwin Cruikshank rang out — into the air, or only in my head?

'*It is your God not mine who says the sins of the fathers shall be visited upon the sons. You have proved yourself an ally, Thomas Neville, and you shall have your reward.*'

'Here we are, soldier-boy, I've made you a cup too.'

Megan limped back into the room, leaning

heavily on her walking stick with one hand and bearing a small tray with three cups on it in the other. 'Hell's teeth!' she said. 'You both look as though you really need this. What *have* you two been talking about?'

22

Leila lay slumped on her pillows as if exhausted. She rallied at the sound of Megan's voice. 'There *was* something troubling me,' she said languidly. 'But I feel better now I've got it off my chest.'

There was so much I wanted to ask her, but it would have to wait until we were alone. And somewhere else, well away from the priory! Cruikshank's presence was everywhere in this crumbling old edifice, lurking in the crypt, hiding in the shadowy corners of the chapel, and most certainly here, in the refurbished wing he had made his home.

And he seemed to be watching over Leila!

Abraham Clegg whips her, I hear the Satanist's voice pronouncing him a dead man and he's shot by Archie Fowler. I show her kindness and I'm told I'm to be rewarded.

The very last thing I wanted was any favours from the person or thing responsible for the death of my dear friend, Tobias Bloom and the near downfall of my family, but for all that I was intrigued to know the form his reward was likely to take.

There was sudden commotion outside, the

sound of shouting, and then a gunshot followed by an awful silence. I rushed out of the room and down the corridor to the main entrance.

The sight that greeted me when I opened the door would have been comical, had it not been for the look of sheer terror on the face of the young cleric standing petrified before a pistol aimed at his vitals by a very determined looking Fowler.

Coggins was at Fowler's side; his pistol was pointing to the ground so I guessed it was his that I had heard being discharged.

Hearing the door open, the big man turned towards the sound. 'He was skulking out there in the trees, Major,' he said, indicating their trembling captive with his empty pistol. 'I put one over his head and told him if he didn't come forward and show himself, the next shot would be aimed straight at him.'

The young man was very thin, with a veritable beak of a nose and lifeless black hair, which, together with the clerical black of his garb and his long spindly legs gave him an almost birdlike appearance. Fear had drained the colour from his face and he stood cowering before his captors twisting his long fingers together nervously.

'We thought 'e were one o' them Cleggs come back,' Fowler added without taking his

260

eyes off his prisoner.

The young man's gaze flitted between the pistol and me. 'I meant no harm, sir, truly I didn't,' he blurted out.

'I think you can put up your weapon, Fowler. Unless I'm mistaken, this gentleman is the curate from Marton.'

A ghost of a smile hovered on the cleric's bloodless lips. 'Indeed I am, sir,' he said gratefully. 'Jeremiah Parrott, at your service.

Thank God Giles wasn't here. For had he been present when a man with such a nose declared his name to be Parrott, he would have doubled up with laughter. Struggling to keep my face straight, I offered him my hand and introduced myself as Thomas Neville.

'*Sir* Thomas Neville of Dunmere Hall?' he said enthusiastically.

I still found the title a trifle embarrassing. I smiled and nodded my head. 'Please forgive my men, Mr Parrott. I posted them here to guard someone who was recently the victim of a most brutal attack. Seeing you in the woods, they thought the assailants had returned.'

'Oh, I quite understand,' he said, effusively. 'It's my fault really for being afraid to leave the protection of the trees. I vowed I'd never visit this place again, but today I suddenly felt an overwhelming compulsion to see its wonderful columned façade, just once more.

Had I known you were here I wouldn't have been worried.'

'About the phantom chorister you mean?'

The young cleric flinched. 'How do you know about that?' he asked.

'Word gets around in a small community,' I said with a reassuring smile. 'You heard chanting right enough, Mr Parrott, but it was nothing more than an attempt by someone who shouldn't have been here to keep inquisitive folk away . . . And don't worry about him, he's been dealt with. Shall we go inside?'

Although my time was limited (I still had to confront Emily), I felt the least I could do, after the fright my retainers had given him, was to offer the man some refreshment.

'So, Mr Parrott, you are something of a scholar?' I said conversationally.

We were seated in the kitchen with a steaming mug of Megan's camomile tea apiece. The sentries were back on duty and Welsh Meg had gone to talk to Leila, so we were alone.

I studied the man sitting opposite me at the big kitchen table. That he was intelligent and well educated I had no doubt but he struck me as the archetypal odd man out, a person who much preferred his own company to that of anyone else.

He looked up from his beverage and smiled

shyly. 'That's possibly something of an exaggeration, Sir Thomas. Some things interest me that's all, ecclesiastical architecture being one of them.'

Purely out of politeness, I said, 'You have other interests, then?'

'Indeed I do, sir,' he replied enthusiastically. 'As a priest, I am, of course, well versed in the history of Christianity, but certain facts about it fascinate me. Did you know, for example, that Abyssinia is the second oldest Christian country in the world?'

I experienced a sudden cold shiver. The saying, 'someone walked over my grave' came to mind, and I wished it hadn't. 'What can you tell me about Abyssinia?' I heard myself asking.

The curate's eyes shone. 'In the twelfth century, Portuguese explorers found a lost Christian civilization on the eastern horn of Africa,' he said excitedly. 'They called it Abyssinia. It lay on a vast plateau surrounded by the lands of Muslims and pagans. It is a country of regions, each ruled over by a prince who, in turn, answers to a king who can trace his ancestry back to the Queen of Sheba and King Solomon. It is a land of strange creatures and vast riches and still attracts adventurers and fortune hunters.

My darling Ayana was a Princess among

women. Josh's words came back to me and a devious plan began to form in my mind.

I looked at my watch. It was time to go and I stood up. 'That's very interesting, Mr Parrott, I'm most grateful to you for that information. I have to leave you now but I'll have one of my men show you round the priory.' He started to rise. 'Do stay and finish your tea,' I said, placing a restraining hand on his shoulder. 'I look forward to our next meeting.'

On my way to the priory's main entrance door I stopped at the bedroom to say goodbye to Leila and to tell Megan I was leaving.

'If you want a ride home on my horse you'd better come now,' I told her, snatching up a cushion from a chair by the door.

She gave me a bewitching smile. 'What did I say about being born lucky?' she purred.

Outside I detailed Fowler to be the curate's guide. 'Just show him the chapel and let him walk round the cloisters. I'll leave the crypt up to you but Leila's quarters are strictly out of bounds, understood?'

He wasn't too pleased at the prospect and went off grumbling. 'Bleedin' toffs should have better things to do with their time. I shouldn't 'ave left the bleedin' army.'

Megan came hobbling out leaning heavily

264

on her stick. I didn't have time to walk my horse back to her cottage; this time it would be me in the saddle.

'The lady is riding pillion, Coggins,' I said, throwing him the cushion. 'Sit her on that.' I put my foot in the stirrup iron and swung up onto the horse's back. 'You'll have to sit astride,' I told her, 'and hang on tight.'

Coggins lifted Megan by the waist as if she was a child and placed her gently on the horse behind me.

'This I like,' she said, her arms sliding round my waist and her face coming to rest between my shoulder blades.

And so, with the Welsh witch, her skirts up around her middle once again and her arms wrapped tightly around me, I set off for Goostrey at a fast trot. We didn't speak on the journey. I was too occupied with my thoughts, and Megan with holding on. Arriving at her isolated cottage, I cocked my leg forward over the saddle horn and slid down. I then lifted her from the horse. As I held her in my arms, still breathless and trembling from the ride, she looked up at me and in a husky whisper, said, 'Why don't you tarry awhile, soldier-boy?'

Had I more time I could easily have succumbed to her charms. As it was, after seeing her safely indoors, I galloped off to Dunmere Hall. I went there directly without stopping at Seth Napper's tavern. I had no need to, I had decided on my stratagem.

Finch and Hagar were at their station on the far side of the moat bridge. Swinging down from my horse, I handed him the reins, telling him I would be in immediate need of both him and the chaise, and ran to the house. I barely had time to bathe and dress for dinner.

When I got to my room I found Nolan there. He had prepared my bath and was busy laying out the clothes I would wear for the evening.

He greeted me with: 'You're cutting it a bit fine, sir, so y'are. If you don't mind me saying so.'

'I've had rather a busy day, Nolan,' I said, collapsing in a chair and lifting a leg for him to pull off my boot. 'I want you to cut along to Finch. Tell him he's to dress in the Neville livery and take the chaise to the tavern to pick up Miss Emily. I'd like you to go with him and if he has a spare livery coat that will fit you, wear it . . . Impress on Finch that Miss Emily is to be treated like royalty. Like royalty, understand?'

Nolan raised an eyebrow but said nothing more than, 'I'll do that, sir,' and after pulling off the other boot, left me to my ablutions.

After the quickest bath I'd ever taken, I

hurriedly dressed and went downstairs. Giles and Mother were standing by the fire in the great hall enjoying a glass of wine before going through to dinner. Lady Neville was a strikingly handsome woman who this evening looked positively regal in a gown made of silk, the yarn spun, no doubt, in Macclesfield and the garment made in Spitalfields, the thought whisking my thoughts back to Ensign Lacoste and the Huguenots.

She saw me approaching and smiled. 'Ah, Thomas,' she said. 'Now you're here we can go in.'

I took a deep breath, and said, 'It is not yet eight, Mother. I think we should wait for our guest.'

It was now my mother's turn to raise an eyebrow. 'A *guest*, Thomas?' Then, as realisation dawned, she scowled and said, 'Don't tell me you've gone ahead and invited that tavern girl? I told you, Thomas, I'll not dine with a serving wench.'

Giles seemed to be enjoying this and stood to one side nodding with the corners of his mouth turned down in a now-you've-done-it look.

'Would you dine with a princess, Mother?' I said.

She scoffed. 'A princess? What nonsense is this, Thomas?'

Lying doesn't come easy to me but I could see neither rhyme nor reason in judging a person by their social background. I've met beggars who were poets and earls that were dunderheads. A person should be judged by what they are, not like a racehorse by their pedigree.

'Emily's mother came from Abyssinia, the second oldest Christian country in the word,' I said, quoting the Reverend Parrott, and with my fingers crossed tightly behind my back, I continued with, 'It's a country of principalities, rather like Germany. Emily's father was a prince who was killed by an ambitious neighbour. Her mother escaped and was brought here by an English explorer. He gave her a position in his household as companion to his wife.'

I paused. Both my mother and Giles were staring at me, open-mouthed. Mother rallied herself and spoke. 'But she married Joshua Napper, and he was penniless when he came to Goostrey?' she said incredulously.

'Of course she had no money. She barely escaped with her life. Napper was the son of the tenant farmer on the explorer's home farm. They fell in love and were married. Then, when Emily was still a child, tragically her mother died in a plague that swept through that part of Derbyshire. Napper buried his wife and left everything to come here to find work.'

Giles grinned. 'So, if Emily's the daughter of a princess, that makes her a princess too!'

'Precisely. Now Mother, I'll ask you again — would you dine with a princess?'

My mother closed her eyes and smiled to herself. I could guess she was relishing telling Mistress Bottomley that she'd had a princess to dinner. I doubt if even Lady Arabella Warblington had had royalty at her table.

Then, giving me a stern look, she said, 'You are absolutely sure about this, Thomas?'

My fingers ached from being crossed. 'As sure as I can be, Mother. It's what I've put together from information I've gathered from a number of sources including Seth Napper himself — and the new curate at Marton, who is something of an authority on Abyssinia . . . There's just one thing I would ask of both of you.'

Giles moved closer. He didn't believe me, I could tell.

'Please don't say anything to Emily,' I said. 'Talking about her mother would only upset her.'

My mother, who was now savouring the thought of being the envy of her social circle and obviously wanted to believe me, said, 'Of course not, dear. The poor woman, after escaping to freedom and finding happiness with a good man, to be cruelly taken like that, and with a little child too.' She dabbed her eyes theatrically with her handkerchief. 'Do you think your father knew, and that's why he didn't hesitate to give Napper the tenancy?'

Lying to my mother was becoming a strain. 'He certainly knew Napper's wife was dead and he was left with a little mouth to feed . . .'

I got no further because at that moment there was the sound of a carriage outside and Smallwood came hurrying through the great hall on his way to the door.

Emily looked lovely in a simple cotton dress. She usually wore her long, black, curly hair pulled back and tied with a ribbon. Tonight it was piled on top of her head, emphasising her long, slender neck. Nolan stood behind her looking mildly embarrassed in a borrowed livery coat that was a little too short in the sleeve. He wore it unfastened, no doubt because it was also too small to button across his broad chest.

I watch my mother advance towards our guest praying that she wouldn't curtsy, and breathing a sigh of relief when all she did was to hold out her hands and say effusively, 'How *lovely* to meet you, my dear. I've been *so* looking forward to this evening.'

Giles looked at me and rolled his eyes.

I was on tenterhooks all evening but looking back I have to say the dinner went well. The two ladies chatted away together like old friends, with Emily proving more than capable of holding her own on any subject my mother cared to introduce. She also impressed me by being able to come up with clever responses to my little brother's witticisms. As usual, I said little but it didn't seem to matter.

When the time came for Emily to leave, I walked her out to the waiting carriage.

'Oh Thomas, it's been a lovely evening,' she said effusively. 'I know your brother almost as well as I know you but I've never been in your mother's company before. She is such a sweet person!'

I smiled grimly, and because Finch and Nolan were present I limited myself to a brotherly peck on the cheek before helping her into the chaise.

When I re-entered the great hall, I found my mother waiting for me by the staircase. 'Blood will out, Thomas!' she exclaimed haughtily. 'Joshua Napper may have diluted the blood royal, but you only have to look at the girl to know she is from noble stock.'

And she had more to say as we climbed the stairs together.

'If she *must* work for her father, Thomas, you'll have to tell him to employ her somewhere away from the public eye. The sooner folk disassociate her with the tavern the better. Why your father allowed Mr Napper to sell strong ale in his farmhouse, I'll never know. I hear tell there's even a female entertainer there now. The place is turning into a veritable bawdy-house.'

23

I went to bed with my conscience bothering me. I lay awake, staring into the darkness of my room for what seemed an age. When I did eventually drift off to sleep I had a most disturbing dream.

Cruikshank was in it, just as he was when I first saw him, nauseatingly handsome with his cold, ice blue eyes, a straight nose above lips that were almost feminine in their sensuality. I remember thinking at the time that he reminded me of the satyr in the huge painting in the long gallery at home — the one I had always hurried past as a child.

Then, suddenly, we were no longer in the tavern but alone, just the two of us, in the crypt at the priory and he *was* that satyr, the horns, the cloven hooves, the lot. And he was smiling at me triumphantly.

'You longed for your sweetheart to be accepted in society,' he said, his voice smooth as velvet, *'and I showed you a way. You took it and in doing so you broke one of your God's commandments, 'Thou shalt not bear false witness.' And that, Thomas Neville, makes you mine!'*

Then he laughed, a long, loud, hollow laugh that echoed in the dark recesses of the underground chamber. As it did, he underwent a further metamorphosis, this time becoming a tall giant of a man with wild, staring eyes and hair that hung down to his shoulders in long greasy tendrils.

I awoke and sat up. I was sweating. Hagar, sensing something was wrong, came over to the bed and licked my hand reassuringly.

I knew the man from my father's description as the condemned murderer who had stood on the gallows platform with the young Edwin Cruikshank, then the curate of St John's, Knutsford. The cleric was still fervently exhorting him to repent his sins when the executioner released the catch of the trapdoor. At the same moment, the prisoner miraculously broke free of his bonds, and with a cry proclaiming the Devil as his master, he grabbed Cruikshank in a macabre embrace and took the terrified curate with him down into the void, the extra weight snapping his neck audibly, and setting in motion a train of strange and terrible events that culminated in the death of my friend, Tobias Bloom.

* * *

Nolan appeared with my shaving water and a dish of tea. I was pleased to see he was wearing his usual garb. 'Miss Emily looked as though she enjoyed the dinner, sir,' he said cheerfully.

'I believe she did, Nolan. I'll find out later when I see her.'

He set about making up my bed. 'Would you credit her getting on so well with her Ladyship, sir? I'm told they chatted away like old friends all through the meal.'

'Who told you that?'

He winked and touched the side of his nose with a forefinger. 'No names, no pack drill, sir. As they used to say back at the barracks.' He smiled as he plumped up the pillows and set them in place. 'Isn't it today Mr Giles joins the regiment, sir? Mind you, I don't envy him learning the drills. No sir, I don't envy him that at all. Although I'm after thinking it'll probably be a mite easier for the officers because they only have to remember how to give the orders.'

His talk of the army set me thinking. 'Tell me Nolan, are you happy in your work?' I asked.

'I wouldn't wish to work for any other gentleman, sir.'

I took a deep breath and came straight out with it. 'Do you regret leaving the army?'

Nolan didn't answer immediately, concentrating instead on smoothing out the wrinkles in the coverlet. When he was satisfied he straightened up and faced me. 'My job in the twenty-second wasn't very different to what I do here, sir, and an Officers' Mess is very much like an English country house, so it is. I'm quite happy here, but if you were to ask me there's one thing about army life that I miss I'd answer you in one word, sir, so I would, and that word would be 'mates'. That may sound odd to you, sir, and you could, quite rightly, point out that there are a lot of servants in this house, and they're a friendly bunch to be sure. But first and foremost, sir, I'm a soldier, trained to face the enemy shoulder to shoulder with my mates, mates that you trust with your life as they trust you with theirs. There's nothing quite like that here, sir.' He lowered his eyes and moved to the wardrobe. 'Will it be the blue coat today, sir?'

* * *

I went downstairs to the parlour, where Smallwood met me with the news that my mother had already breakfasted and was now in the study writing a letter.

'She wants it delivered to Byley Hall the

276

moment it's finished, sir. I've sent Booth, the under footman, to the stables to inform Finch.'

So, Mother couldn't wait to tell Mistress Bottomley about her *coup* at the dinner table.

'Has my brother been down?'

'Not yet, sir. I understand he's still packing.

'I'll bid Lady Neville good morning before I take breakfast, Smallwood,' I said, ordering Hagar to 'stay' and making for the study door.

Mother was folding the note as I entered, and she readily accepted my offer to seal it for her. 'Thank you, Thomas,' she said, with a sigh of relief. 'I'm sure to burn my fingers with the lighted taper or drip molten wax on the desk. It's one of the things your father always did for me.' She looked up. 'You're very much like him, you know.'

It was a nice, loving compliment but I doubted its accuracy. Like Giles, I suppose I bore a passing physical resemblance to our father but neither of us could be likened to him in temperament. Until, under Edwin Cruikshank's evil influence, he became a gambler and a drunkard, Sir Rupert was a serious and somewhat dour gentleman. A singularly undemonstrative man who never let his emotions show.

I felt more akin to his younger brother, Uncle Reuben, the Colonel of the twenty-second. He was an active and restless person, as demanding of himself as he was of his men. Always ready for action and adventure, the family motto, *fortis fortuna adiuvat*, fortune favours the brave or who dares wins, could have been written for him alone.

My mother's voice shook me out of my reverie. The sweetness had gone and I was back to being the recalcitrant child.

'You must start using this study, Thomas. Your father ran the estate from here and you must do the same.'

Unable to hide my exasperation, I replied with a long, drawn out, 'Yes, Mother,' and went into breakfast.

I didn't linger over my toast and marmalade. The thought of Giles riding off to deeds of derring-do with the twenty-second and me stuck behind a desk totting up ledgers didn't do much for my appetite. I'd given Nolan the task of checking that all was well at the priory, thus freeing me to accompany Giles for part of his journey to Chester. I thought I'd go with him as far as Holmes Chapel and return by way of Napper's tavern, where I planned to dally a while with Emily.

My little brother seemed to be taking a

long time to pack a couple of saddlebags, so with Hagar following eagerly at my heels, I went upstairs to see if he needed a hand. I found him sitting on his bed, still in his dressing gown. He looked up as I entered his room, a gloomy expression on his face. This wasn't like Giles; it wasn't like Giles at all.

'I can't do it, brother,' he said morosely. 'I thought I'd got my life sorted out at last, but I can't do it. Damn it, I don't want to do it!'

'What don't you want to do?'

'I don't want to take up my commission.'

Well, I wasn't expecting that, and, without thinking, I blurted out, 'But it's bought and paid for, and you've got your uniform and all your kit,' which, of course, I regretted as soon as I'd said it.

He held his head in his hands and groaned. 'I know, Tom, but it means going away — and God knows when I'll be back again.'

I sat beside him. 'Cheer up, chum. What happened to the brash young fellow who couldn't wait to promenade along the Chester Rows in his new uniform, turning all the ladies heads?'

'That was before I fell in love with Prudence,' he moaned.

It was all I could to stop myself laughing out loud. My little brother had an eclectic taste in women and fell in and out of love with boring regularity, but I could hardly believe his latest paramour was the horsey Prudence Bottomley. I stood up, racking my brain for something I could say that would jerk him back to his senses. I tried: 'What's Mother going to say?'

'She's all for me staying at home,' he said, which rather took the wind out of my sails.

'You've spoken to Mother about this?'

'Yes. She said I was old enough to decide what I wanted to do with my life.'

On reflection, my mother's reaction didn't surprise me. Giles was still her baby and she was never happy to be parted from him for any lengthy period of time. Also, as he was showing an interest in Prudence, the prospect of adding Bottomley land to the Neville estate was still a possibility.

'You've got to give it a try,' I said firmly. 'You owe it to Uncle Reuben. Remember how pleased he was when you said you wanted to join his regiment, and how proud he was when he introduced you to his officers. You don't want to make him look a fool do you?'

Giles looked at his feet and shook his head.

'Listen, little brother, here's what you do. Report to the barracks and do your training. It only lasts two months, and you'll be given leave at the end of it. Think of it as a test of your love. If, at the end of eight weeks, you still feel the same way about Prudence and she still feels the same way about you, I'll come and see Uncle Reuben myself and get you released. Do you agree?'

Giles looked up at me. His face still wore a serious expression but his eyes were shining. 'Eight weeks isn't long is it?'

'It'll fly past,' I said grimly, remembering my own initial training when I was kept so busy drilling, cleaning and polishing my kit, and practicing loading and firing a musket until I achieved the army's minimum requirement of three shots a minute, that, looking back, one day seemed to merge into another, the whole thing being one continuous blur of activity.

He got to his feet. 'By God, Tom, I'll do it! I'll stop at Byley Hall on my way to Chester and tell Prudence.' Then, grinning mischievously, he added, 'I rather think the idea of putting our love to the test will appeal to her. Very romantic and all that, don't you think?'

'Good man, Giles!' I said, punching him playfully on the shoulder. Two months should be long enough to see if my brother was serious about giving up being a soldier. 'Get yourself dressed and have some breakfast. I'll ride with you as far as Holmes Chapel, but first I've got to go over to the priory. Sir Henry Leyton sent word that the Cleggs are in custody, so Leila Sculley can safely return to her cottage. Don't worry, I'll be back by the time you're packed and ready to leave.'

★ ★ ★

I spotted the tall, black figure of Jeremiah Parrott as soon as I cleared the trees. The curate stood gazing up at the priory's ancient façade, a rapt expression on his thin, emaciated face like some biblical ascetic receiving a vision from heaven. Hagar suddenly ran between my horse's legs who showed his annoyance by snorting at her. The sudden noise caused Parrott to spin round, his narrow shoulders slumping with relief when he recognised me.

'Sir Thomas!' he exclaimed. 'I — I was passing and I just had to have one more look at these exquisite pilasters — your guards said it was all right.'

I couldn't help smiling at this earnest young man. 'You can't get enough of this place, can you?'

'It *is* impressive isn't it? Imagine what it must have been like in all its splendour. But it's not just the building, you understand, it's a feeling I get that these ancient stones still retain some of the pious energy that emanated from all those devout men who lived and worshipped here over the centuries.'

'You said you were passing?'

'Oh, yes,' he said, pointing to a skinny dappled mare standing a few yards away nibbling at the grass. 'I volunteered to take the sacrament to those in the Goostrey almshouses who cannot attend church.'

'Knowing that your route would take you past the priory?' I added, causing him to smile sheepishly. 'Tarry awhile, and if you don't mind going by way of Dunmere Hall, you can ride part of the way with my brother and me.'

His thin face lit up. 'I would be honoured, sir, and most grateful to have your company across the moor. I regret there are some miscreants who have no respect for the cloth. Why, only last week the rural dean was set upon and robbed of his purse.'

Hagar yapped at the curate's mare who did no more than lower its head and neigh loudly at its tormenter, expelling the breath from her great lungs with such force that my spindly-legged dog was forced to take a step backwards. Thereafter the dog eyed the horse suspiciously and refused to budge, so leaving her sitting at the edge of the trees with the horses, and the cleric basking in the ambiance of the priory's frontage, I went to tell Leila it was safe for her to return to her cottage.

'Hie up, Dan, we're on the bleedin' move again,' Fowler shouted to his companion when I told him to make a start on packing her things. ''Ere, 'ave we got to stand guard at Miss Sculley's cottage, Major?'

I was about to go into Leila's room. 'No, that won't be necessary,' I called back. 'All the Cleggs are under lock and key.'

To my delight, Leila was out of bed and sitting in a chair by the fire. Although her face was still pale and drawn, she seemed more her old self in spirit.

'I'm glad you're here, Sir Thomas. My wounds need redressing. My two guardians are kindness itself but I could hardly ask them, could I? And you *have* done it before. The salve Megan left is on the bedside table.'

Without more ado, she stood up, turned her back to me and slipped her loose gown off her shoulders so that it hung down from her waist. Carefully, I unwound the bandage that was wrapped around her body, unable to avoid gasping as once again I viewed the cruel lacerations, the pitiless criss-cross of angry-looking stripes that violated the soft white skin of her back.

To my relief, the cuts appeared clean and with no sign of infection; whatever was in Welsh Meg's salve seemed to be working, as they were healing nicely.

I applied the ointment with the tips of my fingers as gently as I could, but with each touch, her whole body tensed and she made little noises with her mouth as if she were sipping a hot drink. It took a long time but once it was done, I bound the wounds with some strips of clean linen that I found neatly rolled up by the salve, presumably prepared by Megan during her visit. Then, with my help, Leila slipped her arms back into her dress and sank down into the chair with a sigh of relief.

'Don't get too comfortable,' I said. 'You're going home.'

The news put a smile on her face, but then a flicker of fear showed in her eyes. 'There's nothing I'd like more than to be back in my little cottage, but is it safe?' she asked.

'Harwood and the Cleggs are all in custody awaiting trial, so you have nothing to fear from them. Get dressed, madam, I'll have a carriage here for you within the hour.'

On my way out, I told my men to make sure to leave the place clean and tidy. 'Don't forget, I don't own this property — yet!'

I then rode back to Dunmere Hall with Jeremiah Parrott. Hagar trotted beside us, when she wasn't running off to look for rabbits that is.

24

Sergeant Finch relieved us of our mounts, shaking his head at the sight of Jeremiah Parrott's rather emaciated dappled-grey. I asked him if Giles had asked for his horse yet.

'He has indeed, sir, a few minutes ago.'

'The Reverend Parrott and I will be riding with Mr Giles, so we will be requiring our horses again very shortly.'

'I'll have them rubbed down and watered, sir. They'll be ready and waiting for you.'

Entering the great hall, Hagar made straight for the fireplace and stretched out in front of the hearth. Parrott took a few paces, then stopped and looked around.

'This is magnificent,' he whispered reverently. 'Just look at the workmanship in that vaulted ceiling . . . '

Smallwood appeared as if by magic. I sent him to tell my brother that I was waiting and ready to leave.

'And the plasterwork on the chimney piece, the delicacy of the detail. Would that be a royal coat of arms?'

My mother answered Parrott's question from the parlour doorway. 'It would, young man,' she said, sweeping into the great hall. 'The arms are that of Her Majesty Queen Elizabeth, put there by Sir John Neville, the first baronet. It was the custom in his day to show the family's allegiance to the crown in the main reception room.' She turned to me. 'Thomas, pray introduce me to our guest.'

Had my mother been Good Queen Bess herself, Parrott couldn't have made a deeper bow. While I was making the introductions, Giles came down the stairs resplendent in his regimentals, closely followed by Nolan carrying his bulky saddlebags.

On seeing him, my mother clapped her hand to her mouth and her eyes filled with tears.

'I'm riding with Giles as far as Holmes Chapel, Mother,' I said hastily. 'The Reverend Parrott is accompanying us as far as Goostrey. He is to administer the sacrament to the housebound at Father's almshouses.'

'Pray forgive me for appearing a little emotional, Mr Parrott,' Mother said, dabbing her cheeks with her handkerchief. 'But, as you see, my darling son is off to be a soldier.'

I don't remember her crying when my father announced that I was to join the army, but then I was only the middle son. Ned, the eldest, heir to the title and estate, occupied most of my father's time and Mother doted on Giles, her youngest, who, in her eyes, would always be her baby.

It was her idea for Giles to be a priest. Her goal was for him to have a cosy local parish, perhaps even St Luke's on the Neville estate, but it didn't work out. Giles lived for the here and now and never gave a thought to the hereafter. He had now decided to join the army and I wondered how long that would last. There would be no question about his loyalty, or his bravery should it be put to the test, but would the free spirit within him resign itself to the privations and harsh discipline of army life? I doubted it.

'What d'you think Tom,' he shouted. 'Will I pass muster?'

'Very smart, little brother. Nolan himself couldn't get a better shine on a pair of boots,' I said, giving my valet a knowing wink. 'Come on, if you're to be in Chester for dinner we'd best be on our way.'

I disentangled Giles from Mother's emotional embrace only to get outside and find Parrott rooted in front of the carving on the parlour window.

'But look, the workman has cut an inscription,' he argued as I attempted to drag him away, and proceeded to read it out loud. *'HAROLD HILL, CARPENTER, MADE THIS WINDOW BY THE GRACE OF*

GOD ... Praise the Lord! Now there's a man who recognised that skill is a gift from Heaven.'

Giles grasped the opportunity to delay his leaving. 'I've often thought he must have been something of a rarity,' he threw in. 'That window dates from the sixteenth century. I wouldn't have thought there were many literate carpenters in those days. What do you think, Tom?'

'I think you won't get to Chester before nightfall if you don't get a move on,' I said.

With Hagar trotting beside me (and I'd swear she had a puzzled look in her eyes), I managed to shepherd my reluctant fellow travellers into the stable yard. As Finch had promised, our horses were ready and waiting for us but there was no sign of our head groom.

Nolan was busily strapping the saddlebags to Giles' mount. When asked if he knew where Finch was, he replied, 'The chestnut gelding cast a shoe so he took it to Goostrey.'

'Why the sudden urgency?' I said, giving voice to my thoughts. 'The smith is a regular visitor to our stables.'

Nolan grinned. 'If you ask me, I think he rather fancied the idea of waiting in the tavern while the horse is attended to.'

'That's where I'm going after I've seen my

brother as far as the Chester Road. If I should miss him, tell him I want him to take the wagon to the priory and convey Miss Sculley and her belongings back to her cottage on the Swettenham road.' I hoisted myself up into the saddle. 'I think you should go too, Nolan, to see that the rooms in the priory are left clean and tidy — and make sure it's locked up when you leave . . . And tell Coggins and Fowler to come back here. Miss Sculley is in no danger now the Cleggs are in custody.'

* * *

After saying goodbye to Giles, off to the twenty-second's barracks in Chester (by way of Byley Hall), I rode back to Goostrey, to the tavern, to see Emily.

When I entered the taproom I found the fire burning merrily in the hearth but the place was empty, which was most unusual for this time of day. Hagar was just settling herself by the burning logs as Josh appeared at the kitchen door. He was not his usual smiling self.

'Oh, it's you, Sir Thomas,' he said. 'I thought I heard someone come in. What can I get you?'

'I'm here to see Emily. Perhaps you'll be kind enough to tell her I'm here, and I'll have a tankard of your excellent ale while I'm waiting.'

His face took on a grim smile. 'The ale I can get you, sir, but Emily I cannot. She's taken the gig and gone off to the priory to see Leila.'

He turned to fill a jug from one of the barrels behind him. 'How is the girl, Sir Thomas? Trade has been real bad without her. Old Scrivens, who has that place down on the London road, saw how Leila was packing 'em in and straight away went and got himself a singer, and now he's taken all my custom.'

'She's much better, although I doubt if she will be strong enough to return to work for some time.'

Josh placed a foaming tankard in front of me with a sigh. Feeling that a change of subject was needed, I said, 'I was rather expecting to see Sergeant Finch here. Have you seen him today?'

'I've not set eyes on Sebastian for days, sir,' he answered grumpily. 'He's probably taken to drinking at Scrivens' place like the rest of 'em.'

Josh excused himself and went back to the kitchen, leaving me feeling that unless he pulled himself together he'd drive away the few customers who did still drop in. I took my ale to a seat by the fire. If Finch had intended waiting here for the horse he would have been here by now. Perhaps he had other business in Goostrey?

In spite of his gloomy mood Josh Napper still brewed exceptionally good ale but on this occasion I limited myself to the one tankard. Hagar was loath to leave the warmth of the fire but dragged herself away when she saw I was serious about leaving. We then walked across the road to the smithy.

If Josh's taproom was warm, there it was hot! Benson, the brother of the Neville estate's bailiff, was working the bellows of the forge with one hand while with the other he gripped the long tongs in which he held a glowing red strip of metal amid the blazing coals. Sweat beaded his brow and ran in rivulets down his brawny arms.

Taking the bar out of the fire and holding it on the horn of the anvil he began hammering it into shape. It was then that he noticed me. He stopped. 'Sir Thomas,' he said, surprised. 'I'm afraid the gelding isn't ready. I'm just making a shoe for it now.'

'Don't let me stop you, Benson. It's Finch I'm after, not the horse. Can you tell me where he's gone?'

'He didn't say, sir, but it shouldn't be far. He left his horse here.'

Benson turned to put the piece of metal

back in the fire and I walked away. Where could Finch have gone? Was he on an errand for Cook, or Smallwood?

I tried the bakery, the butcher, even Colclough's carpentry workshop, all without success. I was now at the edge of the village, not far from Welsh Meg's cottage.

He wouldn't, would he?

Well, there was only one way to find out. I walked up the short path and knocked on the door. I wasn't kept waiting long before the door opened and Megan was standing there, a devilish twinkle in her eye and a ghost of a smile playing around her captivating lips.

'Soldier-boy!' she exclaimed. 'What a nice surprise. Come in. Come in. You're my second visitor today from Dunmere Hall.'

She ushered me into her living room, and there he was, sitting on a chair by the fire, looking like a little boy caught with his hand in the biscuit jar. Hagar made straight for him and nuzzled his leg.

'I'll make us all a nice cup of tea,' Megan announced happily and disappeared into her tiny kitchen, leaving me alone with my old tutor.

'It's not what you think, Master Thomas,' he said firmly. 'I came here for some of Welsh Meg's horse liniment. Wonderful stuff it is for reducing swellings and easing irritations. I

293

dunno what she puts in it other than St John's wort and comfrey, but it certainly does the trick.'

I gave him a knowing smile. 'I don't doubt it, Finch. And whatever else you came for is none of my business.'

He threw a cushion at me just as Megan re-entered the room. 'Now, boys, behave. You're not at home now,' she chided.

Over tea I told Finch to hitch up the wagon when he got back to the Hall and take it across to the priory. 'I'd like you to take Leila Sculley back to her cottage,' I explained, adding, 'I've told Nolan he's to go with you.'

Megan left us again and returned with two corked bottles, one a large wine bottle, the other a small phial. 'Here we are, gentlemen. Here's the liniment, Sebastian,' she said handing Sergeant Finch the large bottle. 'And this is for you, soldier-boy.'

With that, she placed the small cylindrical container in my hand.

'I didn't ask you for anything,' I protested. 'What's this?'

She gave me a bewitching smile. 'I know you didn't,' she purred. 'But you *need* this. It's a decoction of Aspen. Take a sip of it the next time you are with Emily, and swill it around your tongue. Trust me, it will make *all* the difference.'

Finch and I took our leave of the mysterious and enchanting Megan Griffith and parted company at her gate, Finch striding off to Benson's smithy and me to Josh's tavern where I had left my horse. Now that Finch had his instructions I was free to ride out to the priory and meet up with Emily. For a moment Hagar wasn't sure whom to follow but ultimately decided to stay with me.

A most unusual sight greeted me when I turned into the tavern's stable yard. I was quite used to seeing Josh Napper driving his farm wagon but there was something about him on horseback that put me in mind of a Toby Jug, that increasingly popular table piece the Ralph Woods' Burslem pottery were turning out by the dozen.

'Well met, Sir Thomas,' he shouted. 'I'm off to escort my Emily home. I don't like the thought of a young lass riding across the heath on her own. Milly Goodrich can easily take care of what trade there's likely to be in the tavern.'

'I can save you the trouble, Napper. I'm about to do the very same thing.'

'What say we ride together, sir?' he ventured, a broad smile on his rosy-cheeked face. ''Tis a fine day and I'd enjoy your company.'

We trotted off together along the lanes, commenting on the beauty of the autumn colours in the trees and hedgerows, laughing at the antics of Hagar sticking her head down every rabbit hole she could find and at one particularly brainless cock pheasant who seemed intent on committing suicide by darting under our horses hooves.

Our laughter died in our throats when we reached the crossroads. The gibbet was creaking under the weight of a new occupant.

'That's Jolly Roger Bagshaw,' Josh commented sagely. 'The stupid young fool accepted a wager that he'd rob the Manchester stagecoach and got shot by the guard for his pains. The ball struck him in the shoulder. It's a pity it didn't finish him, it would've saved the hangman a job ... I wonder who his visitor is?'

The body, wound with chains, swung gently in the breeze that blew across the heath. Before it, stood a dark figure, head bowed and hands together in prayer, and a few yards off a dappled-grey horse nibbled the grass. I recognised the horse instantly and so apparently did Hagar who shot across the road and began yapping at the horse's legs, from a safe distance.

'That will be the Reverend Jeremiah Parrott, the curate of Marton church,' I said.

'I'll introduce you.'

Consequently, when the good Mr Parrott learned of our destination, I wasn't surprised to find myself with another companion on the short ride to the priory.

'I never did get a good look at the chapel, Sir Thomas,' he said, as Coggins and Fowler led our horses away to where Emily's gig was tethered. 'My guide seemed loath to enter it, so I had to content myself with the view from the doorway. He said there was nothing much to see but it's my guess he'd heard all those wild stories about the Black Mass being celebrated there.'

'Oh, it was right enough,' I said, remembering the night my little band and I had interrupted the sinister ritual to rescue my mother.

The five-pointed star with its strange mystic symbols was just as Edwin Cruikshank had painted it on the floor of the chancel and the black candles and inverted crucifix still stood on the altar.

Josh Napper made straight for Leila's bedroom and, by the sound of girlish laughter as he opened the door, had found his daughter with her friend. I excused myself from the eager young cleric, telling him to go ahead and look around the chapel.

Take all the time you want,' I said. 'I'll join

you as soon as I've attended to the matters that brought me here.

The bedroom, with its wood panelled walls, heavy drapes and dark furniture, could easily be a gloomy place but today a fire burned merrily in the hearth and Leila had pulled the curtains right back to make the most of what sunshine there was. That, and the girls' animated conversation, made it a most cheerful place to walk into. I was amazed by Leila's apparent recovery as she was actually teaching Emily some new dance steps. Their laughter was the result of trying to persuade a reluctant Josh to take part.

'Ah, another gentleman,' Leila cried. 'Now we each have a partner.'

'Oh, no,' I said with a laugh, evading her clutching hands. What I wanted was a few moments alone with Emily but I felt obliged to rescue the fat tavern keeper. 'Napper, I've left the Reverend Parrott in the chapel. Tell him I'll not keep him long, will you?'

Josh gave me a grateful wink as he made for the door, almost colliding with Fowler who was looking for me to announce the arrival of the farm wagon.

I told him to fetch Coggins and damp down the fires and when that was done they were to load everything we had brought with us from Leila's cottage.

The news had brought the dancing class to an end and Leila began gathering up the few small possessions that remained unpacked. There was nothing for Emily to do and she stood there looking lost. I suggested we wait outside. This was the moment I'd been hoping for. I had made one of the most important decisions of my life. Whether I acted upon it or not depended on Emily's answer to a question I was about to put to her.

I stepped outside to be greeted by an excited Hagar who had obviously worked out that as Parrott's horse was tethered it wasn't an immediate danger.

Finch was in the process of turning the wagon around. Nolan had jumped down and was waiting for the old cavalryman to complete the manoeuvre. I beckoned to him and he ran over and stood to attention in front of me. Old habits die hard, I thought, which, in view of what I had in mind, made me smile.

'Pack up all the food that's in the kitchen and stow it in the wagon,' I told him. 'Then, when everyone has gone, I want you to go through the place making sure it's clean and tidy and all the doors are locked. I don't want any complaints from Sir Vivian.'

'Do I have to go down into the crypt, sir?'

he asked, looking decidedly uneasy.

'No. You don't even have to go into the chapel, just the living accommodation. Is that all right?'

'That'll be fine, sir, so it will,' he said. 'There's just one other thing, sir. I came here with Sergeant Finch in the wagon . . .'

'You can take my horse. I'll be going back in the gig with Miss Napper.'

Emily pricked up her ears. 'You're most welcome to ride with me, Thomas, but I shall be stopping at Leila's cottage on my way home, to see her settled in.'

'That's perfect,' I replied. 'It, er, fits in with my plans admirably.'

'I suppose you'll want to drive,' she said, pouting her lips and pretending to sulk.

Knowing that a gig is notoriously easy to overturn, I said a silent prayer and replied, 'Er, not at all. If you want to drive, you go ahead.'

Nolan and Finch had gone into the priory so, for a limited period of time, we were alone. It was now or never.

'Emily.'

She turned and smiled at me. 'Yes?' she said, brightly.

'I, er, um.' God, this was awful. 'I'm, er, that is . . .'

Coggins and Fowler appeared carrying the

bedding out to the wagon. I waited until they had gone. 'I'm going back into the army,' I said.

The smile was replaced by a frown. 'But you gave up the army to come looking for me,' she said, pouting her lips. 'And now I'm found you're off to play soldiers again? Really, Thomas, you are too much!'

She turned her head away, but not before I saw her eyes beginning to fill with tears. Should I take her in my arms or would that frighten her away? I hung my head and shrugged my shoulders, digging my hands deep into the pockets of my coat, trying to put together the words that needed to be said. The whole of my future pivoted on the next few moments. I had to get it right.

The fingers of my right hand encountered an object in the pocket. It was the phial that Megan had given me. 'Trust me', she had said. Very well, I had nothing to lose. I took the phial out of my pocket and after faking a cough, I tipped its contents into my mouth, rolling the syrup around my tongue as Megan had directed. Its taste was not unpleasant. I waited, not knowing what I was waiting for.

25

There was a group clustered around the wagon that was now loaded with the blankets and pillows we had brought from Leila's cottage. Nolan had appeared first with a large hamper, which he proceeded to strap on the tailboard. Finch came next helping Leila out and fussing over her like a mother hen, carefully settling her into the vehicle before climbing up on the driving seat. The arrival of Fowler and Coggins completed the muster. Nolan broke away and came over to where I was standing with Emily.

'All ready to go, sir,' he said. 'I'll hang on to make sure everything's ship-shape before I lock up. Do you need to go back in for anything, sir?'

Emily flounced off towards the gig. I told Nolan, 'No,' and waved him away with, 'Carry on,' the well-used military phrase that covers every eventuality — and hurried after her.

'How can you do this to your dear sweet Mama?' Emily said petulantly, unhitching her horse and stroking its nose. 'With both her sons away, who will look after the estate?'

'Norbury will continue to oversee the

302

running of both the Hall and the estate as he has done since my father's death,' I said. 'In this he will be assisted by his two able lieutenants, Smallwood the butler and Benson the bailiff. I have set up a fund with my bankers into which Norbury will deposit all rents and from which he will pay the monthly bills. All my mother will be required to do is discuss the daily menu with Cook . . . Anyway, I don't expect Giles to be away that long. He'll do his basic training and then he'll come home and marry Prudence Bottomley.'

'You mean he'll give up the army?'

'Not entirely. He'll probably attend dining-in nights and do the odd annual camp — just enough to allow him to keep the uniform and wear it when it suits him.'

She turned to face me, her pretty mouth set in a determined line. 'You've got this all planned out, haven't you, Thomas?'

'I have,' I said. 'But it will only work with your consent.'

'My consent? Consent to what?'

'To come with me — as my wife.'

Her eyes widened in surprise. 'Thomas Neville, you are the most unromantic person I've ever met!'

'But I've just asked you to marry me!'

'I know you have, you silly goose,' she said with a laugh. 'And I will, I will. But why don't you simply tell me you love me?'

'I could climb the highest mountain and shout it to the heavens,' I said, 'but the wind would blow my words away. I could run down to the sea and write it in big letters in the sand, but the tide would wash it away. No, my dearest, the words, 'I love you', are written on my heart for all eternity.'

Emily fell into my arms with a little sob of delight and I said a silent thank you to Megan for whatever it was she had put in that phial.

The wagon looked to be all loaded up and ready to leave. Sergeant Finch walked over to the gig. 'I'm going now, sir. Will you be following with the young lady?'

'That's the plan, Finch. Off you go.'

He touched a finger to his brow and was about to turn away when he remembered something. 'Oh, by the way, sir,' he said. 'Welsh Meg gave me a message for you.'

'Really, what is it?'

'The name of the elixir she gave you, sir. She said I wasn't to tell you until after you had met up with Miss Emily, Lord knows why.'

'Come on, Finch. Out with it, man!'

'She said it's called, 'Jacob's cork', sir. That's a rum name, isn't it? I hope it did the trick.'

The conniving witch, I thought. 'It certainly did, Finch, it certainly did,' I said, and with a happy smile on my face and my arm around my intended I watched him walk away.

Emily brought me back to reality with, 'As we are travelling together, how are you getting back to the Hall?'

'I'll borrow a nag from your father,' I said. And then I remembered. 'Your father! I'd quite forgotten him! He's still in the chapel with Jeremiah Parrott. I'll have to rescue him. Stay there, I won't be long'

It was cold in the chapel and I could hear Parrott's voice droning on. I walked down the aisle feeling terribly guilty for leaving Josh Napper exposed to the enthusiastic young cleric's academic lecturing but instead of finding the fat tavern keeper slumped in a pew looking bored to death he was on his feet and appeared to be listening intently to what he was being told. On hearing my approach, the talking ceased and they both turned to see who it was interrupting them.

'Ah, Sir Thomas,' Josh said, a broad grin on his rubicund face. 'The reverend is telling me all about Abyssinia.'

With a start, I remembered the conversation I'd had with Parrott on the subject. 'I'm sorry, Napper, I may have inadvertently mentioned to him that your wife . . . '

'Not a problem, sir. What this young man has been telling me is fascinating.'

Parrott gave me a bland smile and turned his attention back to his eager listener. 'Mr Napper,' he said gently, 'you were about to tell me the name of your dear wife's father.'

'I remember it because it were a strange name,' Josh said. 'Ras Giorgis. He came from somewhere called Begem-something.'

'Begemder?'

Josh beamed. 'Yes, Begemder.'

'And it was *Ras* Giorgis?' Parrott asked excitedly.

'Oh yes, definitely 'Ras'. What's so special about that?'

'I'll tell you what's special, Mr Napper,' the curate replied triumphantly. 'Your father-in-law was a prince, that's what! Ras Giorgis, or Prince George, was the ruler of Begemder Province until he was assassinated back in the '30s.'

Josh rubbed his chin. 'Well, that would tie in with when my Ayana came to England right enough.' He chuckled. 'I always said she were a princess.'

So I hadn't told my mother a lie. Emily really *was* a princess. I felt rather pleased about that.

Then, from beneath my feet came a long, drawn-out howl, which began as a cry of anger and tailed off in an echoing wail of despair: 'No-ooooo . . .'

Trust Cruikshank to have the last word.